Downers Grove North HS

P9-BYG-543

DAY
ZERO

DATE DUE

SEP 2 5 2019
OCT 3 1 2019

ALSO IN THE ARCANA CHRONICLES

Poison Princess

Endless Knight

Dead of Winter

Arcana Rising

KRESLEY COLE

DAY ZERO

THE ARCANA CHRONICLES

VALKYRIE PRESS

NEW YORK   BASIN TOWN   STERLING   REQUIEM   FORT ARCANA

Valkyrie Press
228 Park Ave S #11599
New York, NY 10003

This book is a work of fiction. Any references to historical events, real people, or real places are used fictitiously. Other names, characters, places, and events are products of the author's imagination, and any resemblance to actual events or places or persons, living or dead, is entirely coincidental.

Copyright © 2016 by Kresley Cole

All rights reserved, including the right to reproduce this book or portions thereof in any form whatsoever.

ISBN 978-0-9972151-2-0
ISBN 978-0-9972151-3-7 (ebook)

Published in the United States of America.

39905001022974

DEAR READERS,

I initially put together snapshots for each of the Arcana as a guide to help with the screenplay of the Arcana Chronicles.

My goal was to illuminate certain characters' motivations and delve further into their backgrounds.

I've since expanded *Day Zero* into a companion guide, with narratives for most of the players. I omitted villains that were defeated in past books, and for reference, I included Evie's memories of the apocalypse from *Poison Princess.*

This book became one of the most challenging—and rewarding—writing projects I've ever taken on.

Be forewarned: SPOILERS ABOUND. This companion is intended for those who have already read *Poison Princess, Endless Knight,* and *Dead of Winter.*

Some might take Jack's story in *Day Zero* as proof that he's the inactivated card. In fact, I included him because so many have asked for his account of the Flash. I'm neither denying nor confirming whether he is an Arcana. And unfortunately, the Fool redacted information on the one player Jack could be (as well as his own card).

All will be revealed soon.

Thank you for taking this journey with me!

My warmest wishes,
Kresley Cole

ORIGIN OF THE ARCANA

Millennia ago, the gods grew bored.

So Isis, the goddess of magic and wisdom, devised entertainment: a contest to the death for select mortals. She invited gods of other realms to each choose a representative from their most prestigious house, a mortal under the age of twenty-five who would carry the god's emblem into battle.

These players would fight inside Tar Ro (ancient Egyptian for *royal road*), a sacred realm as large as a thousand kingdoms. Isis plagued Tar Ro with disasters to honor various gods and to fuel conflicts between the players.

With each kill, a player would harvest a god's emblem from an opponent, which would then appear on his or her own hand; only the player who collected all the others' emblems would leave Tar Ro alive—as an immortal victor.

Naturally, the deities cheated, gifting his or her representative with superhuman abilities. *Secret* abilities. Thus the players became known as *Arcana*.

A sea god sent the Priestess, a devout girl he blessed with power over all bodies of water. A goddess of learning sought the most brilliant lord from her realm, then struck him mad—to make the Fool unpredictable in the game. An underworld god cursed a young nobleman to kill all he touched, then dispatched his Knight of Death to play.

Nineteen other deities from distant planes sent mortals to almost certain doom.

This vicious Tar Ro game proved so popular with the gods that they decided to host it every few centuries in different lands across the mortal plane until the end of time. . . .

Deprived of their lifeblood—worshippers' prayers—these old deities are thought to have moved on to other worlds, but their legacies live on. On the eve of a new game, each god's magic seeks out a descendant from his or her House of Arcana.

Players are transformed; a new game is dealt.

The earth suffers in their wake.

You may have seen symbols of these games on the face of modern Tarot cards. Each trump card represents a player and contains important clues about his or her past battles, allies, foes, strengths, and weaknesses.

The object of the game: trump every other card by any means necessary, slaying opponents to collect their emblems, now known as icons. In the end, the winner "holding all the cards" will be made immortal until all the others reincarnate to play again.

A prize worth killing for.

And now, in the beginning years of this millennium, a new game has begun along a royal road across a land called North America. . . .

Which of the Arcana will triumph? Can the Hanged Man defeat the electrifying Tower? Will the Priestess's tidal waves extinguish the Emperor's lava? Can the wily Fool outfox them all?

Hail Tar Ro. May the most powerful card kill, and may the best hand win.

THE FLASH

BY THE BOOKS

Arthur's description: Laserlike shafts of sunlight had blasted the earth for the course of one entire global night. Those fields of green cane Evie remembered dreamily would've been charred to ash. Anything organic—any living thing caught outside shelter—was incinerated.

And so many people, transfixed by the pretty lights, had wandered from their homes, drawn like moths to a flame.

As if by design.

Bodies of water flash-evaporated, but no rain has fallen in eight months. All plant life has been permanently destroyed; nothing will grow anew. And only a small percentage of humans and animals lived through the first night.

In the ensuing days, millions more people perished, unable to survive the new toxic landscape.

For some reason, most females sickened and died.

An unknown number of humans mutated into "Bagmen"— contagious zombielike creatures, cursed with an unending thirst and an aversion to the sun.

Some call them hemophagics—blood-drinkers. I believe they are *anything* drinkers, but without water to be found, they've turned to people, walking bags of liquid.

Evie's vision: Night was falling. And across the sky, ethereal lights flickered, crimson and violet, like Mardi Gras streamers. I gaped as flames arced over the school, those eerie lights like a twinkling crown above the fire.

3

Across the grounds, a river of snakes slithered over each other, their scales reflecting the lights above. Panicked rats scurried alongside the creatures that usually ate them.

Those flames descended, searing them to ash, everything to ash.

Flames blazed across a night sky. Beneath the waves of fire, fleeing rats and serpents roiled over Haven's front lawn, until the ground looked like it rippled.

The sun had shone—at night—searing people's eyes till they ran with pus, mutating their bodies and rotting their brains. They became zombielike blood-drinkers, Bagmen, with skin that looked like crinkled paper bags and oozed a rancid slime.

Jack's description to Evie: "Everything's covered in ash, but not every place is burned. Some towns look striped from the lines of flames that hit the ground. Real finger-of-God stuff. One house stands while the one beside it burned down. No rhyme or reason, like how a tornado strikes."

Character Guide

The Major Arcana*

0. The Fool, Gamekeeper of Old (Matthew)	*XI. The Fury, She Who Harrows (Spite)*
I. The Magician, Master of Illusions (Finneas)	*XII. The Hanged Man, Our Lord Uncanny ▮▮▮▮)*
II. The Priestess, Ruler of the Deep (Circe)	*XIII. Death, the Endless Knight (Aric)*
III. The Empress, Our Lady of Thorns (Evie)	*XIV. Temperance, Collectress of Sins (Calanthe)*
IV. The Emperor, Stone Overlord (Richter)	*XV. The Devil, Foul Desecrator (Ogen)*
V. The Hierophant, He of the Dark Rites (Guthrie)	*XVI. The Tower, Lord of Lightning (Joules)*
VI. The Lovers, Duke & Duchess Most Perverse (Vincent & Violet)	*XVII. The Star, Arcane Navigator (Stellan)*
VII. The Centurion, Wicked Champion (Kentarch)	*XVIII. The Moon, Bringer of Doubt (Selena)*
VIII. Strength, Mistress of Fauna (Lark)	*XIX. The Sun, Hail the Glorious Illuminator (Sol)*
IX. The Hermit, Master of Alchemy (Arthur)	*XX. Judgment, the Archangel (Gabriel)*
X. Fortune, Lady of Chance (Zara)	*XXI. The World, This Unearthly One (Tess)*

*Note subtle differences from previously available lists and modern interpretation.

DEATH (XIII)

Aric Domīnija, the Endless Knight, Reigning Arcana Champion
Unspecified call

A.k.a.: The Reaper, Tredici

Powers: Touch of Death (can kill with contact). Death awareness (can sense dead things and approaching death). Superhuman speed, strength, endurance, dexterity, senses, healing. Controlled telepathy.

Special Skills: Gifted horseman, unmatched swordsman.

Weapons: Swords, scythe, his warhorse Thanatos.

Tableau: A Reaper clad in black armor, scythe at the ready, riding a pale horse with evil red eyes. He carries a black flag emblazoned with a white rose.

Icon: Scythe.

Unique Arcana Characteristics: Wears impenetrable armor, spiked gloves, and a helmet. Eyes turn starry with emotion.

Before Flash: A mysterious, reclusive billionaire, securing his mountain compound against any foreseeable disaster.

LETHE CASTLE
DAY 0

Of course *hers* would be the last icon to fade. The rose symbol.

In the shower, I stare at the back of my right hand. Of the twenty-one icons that have marked my skin for so long, only fragments remain of the rose that represented the great Empress's life.

I took this icon when I beheaded her. For centuries, I have stared at it with a mixture of fury, guilt, and yearning.

It connected me to her. My wife.

Whenever the beginning of our lethal game nears, the icons borne by the winner fade. Telepathic Arcana calls start to sound. We are on the brink.

Anticipation strains even my eternal patience. I will capture this new reincarnation of the Empress and make her pay.

At last.

I have waited 677 years, 3 months, and 13 days for this time to come.

Other Arcana have envied my immortality. I would gladly give it up if not for her—my fantasy and nightmare, all wrapped in one.

I have no choice except to win. If I'd died in the past, I would have been reincarnated for another game, losing my memories of her and our history. My soul would have entered a new body, one lacking the warning that I had tattooed over my torso.

Three scenarios might play out in a future game. . . .

I wouldn't go out of my way to find her, missing her entirely.

I would find her, only to kill her before I discovered I could touch her.

Or, worst of all, I would find her, touch her, then *trust* her.

My hands ball into fists, and I hang my head under the stream of water. With the memories I've retained, I've already been able to locate her, and other Arcana as well. They tend to stand out, and in this age of information, I possess every advantage.

To find the Empress, I searched all over the world for farms named Haven. Her home has always been called that. In more than one Arcana chronicle, I've read the advice: "Never attack an Empress in her Haven."

Only one farm of that name has a girl of the right age living on the property. She is a Louisiana teenager named Evangeline *Greene.*

She has no idea that a few states away, she has a husband who plots to destroy her.

I found her social media accounts with pictures of her friends (surprisingly many), her *boyfriend* (a football player who looks as dim as he is handsome), and her home.

The manor at Haven is circled by twelve oaks, like the twelve stars in her Empress crown, and is surrounded by miles of sugarcane in every direction. Strategically genius.

I've also seen pictures of her, this Evangeline Greene. My wife.

She is . . . stunning. Shining golden locks. Merry eyes. Curving lips and cheeks pink with health.

In games past, she had a formidable physical presence, tall and commanding, more Demeter then Aphrodite. In this game, she is all Aphrodite. Comelier than anything I've seen in all my years.

I torture myself imagining what thoughts go on behind those merry eyes. There exists a way for me to know. But what would the clever Fool demand for such a boon?

Even now I hear the Empress's Arcana call. —*Come . . . touch . . . but you'll pay a price.*—

My gut clenches with want. My blood *burns* for her.

I touched, and by all the gods, I've paid.

Naturally, the one game I've vowed not to be seduced, she turns out to be breathtakingly beautiful.

Yet more than her beauty attracts me. She is brimming with *life*; as ever, she calls to me, to Death.

My fist shoots out against the shower tile, shattering it.

In my study at Lethe Castle, I strip off my hated gloves and pour a vodka.

The catastrophe that marks the beginning of each game could happen at any instant, but I've finalized the preparations of Lethe.

My home sits atop an isolated mountain, chosen for its strategic location. Considering the Emperor's powers, I'd made sure the property was some distance from any major seismic activity. With my Empress in mind, I'd selected a site without trees.

Cold-war renovations had already been in place when I bought the castle, and then I outfitted it for whatever catastrophe might befall us now.

Electrical storms? Copper sheets line the walls and ceilings. Flood? We are well above the flood zone. Wildfires? The castle was constructed of flame-proof slate and stone. With the touch of a button, blast-proof shutters will cover all the windows and doors.

Should there be another famine, a subterranean farm with acres of sun lamps will sustain Lethe. Another drought? Sunken reservoirs and wells will provide water.

If marauders actually find this place, a reinforced stone perimeter wall surrounding the entire mountaintop will hinder a raid.

The Arcana players come from all over the world; why should I not believe the scope of the disaster will be global? Communications will go first. I have prepared for that as well.

I possess so many advantages over the others. The deck is eternally stacked in my favor. My allies will benefit as well, at least for a time.

Among the players I've located, I have chosen four.

A Kenya Special Forces soldier named Kentarch is the Centurion, my first ally. His family line has forever named the firstborn son Kentarch. I've messengered a satellite phone to him with instructions to contact me.

Circe Rémire, a Bermudan PhD student obsessed with Atlantean folklore and witchcraft must be the Priestess. Her photo online bears a slight resemblance to her previous incarnation, and she was named for

Circe's Abyss (according to her university bio). Ages ago, the abyss had been named *for her.*

Like me, she has been beguiled and betrayed in the past by the Empress. I've dispatched the Priestess's trident to her. It should accelerate her witchly protection and memory spells.

My third ally will be the Devil. In a small Ohioan gazette, I read an account of a misshapen boy with horns. I will collect him after the disaster. As ever, he will be a vile beast, but he has two advantages. He is immune to the Empress's poison, and his hands will be able to work metal like a forge.

I think of my armor displayed on a stand in my room. Its fit is close, its movements silent. Made from an unidentifiable black ore, the entire suit weighs less than my longswords, as light as it is impenetrable.

This mysterious material can only be reworked by the Devil Card. With each game, I have him update and perfect the armor.

I've already secured my fourth ally. In past months, I'd found stories online about a teenage girl with a remarkable talent for training and rehabilitating dangerous beasts. She had to be the Strength Card, also known as Fauna.

She'd hired out her services, even advertised. In one video, she'd gazed at the camera with clear eyes and chin raised, boldly stating, "My name is Lark Inukai. I defang killers. I defuse their aggression. I find their weaknesses and exploit them ruthlessly. Animals come to me one way and leave another. Do you have a problem case? Call the Killer Chiller."

Even now I shake my head. *Killer Chiller?* There is no accounting for taste.

I hired her father, a veterinarian who'd emigrated from Japan, to oversee my vast collection of animals. Takao and Fauna moved to Lethe Castle a few months ago.

I've given him an unlimited budget to increase our stock. He is currently on his way back from acquiring a rare Russian leopard. As with many of our creatures, some celebrity had purchased it without much forethought.

I exhale. *Mortals.*

I called Takao yesterday and told him to make haste returning. If he doesn't make it back, he could be separated from the safety of the castle when disaster strikes. He could be killed.

All because he couldn't resist the promise of beauty.

A few weeks ago, I told Fauna, "You and your father gravitate toward beautiful animals. Sometimes the spellbinding creatures are the most dangerous ones of all." *Like the Empress.*

Fauna had frowned. "I don't understand."

"In life, you should always steel yourself against anything that is alluring. The next time you see something beautiful, turn away from it." I speak from bitter experience.

Restless, I rise and cross to my wall safe. Combination entered, I open the door to my most valuable treasures. I reach past the necklace I once gave the Empress to collect a small case. Inside is my mother's wedding ring, an engraved gold band with an oval of inlaid amber.

In two out of the last three games, I almost gifted this ring to the Empress. When I married her millennia ago, it had been in safekeeping hundreds of miles away, and I never had the opportunity to retrieve it. In the game after that, the Emperor killed her before I could reach her. In the last game, she'd tried to poison me before I could slip it on her finger.

I take the ring from its case, and the metal warms against my skin. I give a harsh laugh. The ring doesn't know my touch is lethal. It reacts to me as it would to anyone.

So did the Empress's skin.

I recall my last few encounters with her from the previous game— not that I need anything to harden my resolve against her.

All those years ago, I shadowed her, observing her battles, trying to determine whether she was as treacherous as she'd been the last time I'd seen her, when she'd intended to kill me on our wedding night.

She'd been even worse. . . .

"You've stalked me long enough, Reaper. Shall we fight at last?" she asks, looking as if she burns for the battle. Her swirling glyphs glow.

We begin to circle each other.

She cants her head. "The fall sun shines. Chaff spreads on the winds. So much birdsong, music fit for murder. Which one of us will it be?" She is stalling. Her roots are likely spreading beneath me, her serpents at the ready.

But I am invulnerable to them in my armor. "I don't wish to fight today. I only want to converse with you."

"Converse?" She narrows her green eyes. "If that were true, then why are you covered in metal?"

Taking a calculated risk, I remove my helmet, but keep it in hand. "Better?"

Her gaze sweeps from my sword to my helmet. She's assessing her odds. She knows I can cut through her vines with my inhuman speed. Then she studies my face.

I make my expression blank, refusing to show my yearning for a wife, a companion.

"You're a handsome man. Very handsome." Observing how the sunlight strikes my gaze, she murmurs, "With spellbinding eyes."

I stifle my ridiculous flare of pleasure.

"Yet so grim. Is it because you're untouched? Or perhaps a male like you has no wish to be caressed?"

I would do murder for it! *But I say nothing. We continue circling each other.*

"Fitting that we—life and death—should meet in a time of pestilence and famine." She tilts her head, her red locks swaying over a pale shoulder. "Why do you follow me throughout this game, Reaper?"

"To determine your character."

"You've seen me make many kills."

She'd defeated the Lovers before I could reach her, but I'd watched her annihilate humans in a bloodbath, taunting them all the while. At the time, I hadn't known why *she'd lashed out at them. "You attacked those men because they attempted to burn you at the stake. I did not know you sought retribution."*

"They blamed me for their starvation." She shrugs. "They have no idea that I lament the famine as well." It weakens her powers. Each plant is a potential weapon for her. "When I smelled my flesh cooking like a savory leg of venison, I bayed for their blood." Still we circle. "Between the humans and the Arcana, I've been quite busy. And the Emperor must be nearing soon."

"In the last game, he killed you. Gruesomely."

"Unlike when you killed me—cleanly." Her tone is amused.

I incline my head.

"If I recall my chronicles, you defeated the Emperor last," she says, "but in contrast to all the rest of your kills, you tortured him. Why?"

Because he destroyed you before I could get to you. Because I'll never know what might have been. "What would you say if I told you I did it for you?"

She smiles, and it fills me with wariness and lust. "I would say do it again, my Grim Reaper."

"After disappearing for weeks, you are back again?" The Empress's tone is teasing. "Perhaps to converse more?"

I don't remove my helmet this time. I have heard through the Arcana calls that she betrayed one of her staunch allies. "You murdered Fauna in cold blood." Upon the Empress's hand are three icons, those of the Lovers, the Magician, and Fauna.

"No, I defended myself. She and the Magician plotted against me. She attacked with her lions . . . one creature seized my leg in its fangs." She pulls up her skirt to reveal her thigh. "Oh, thank the gods, I have already healed."

My heart begins to thunder at the sight of her bare flesh. Noting my interest, she glides the material higher, as if searching for the wound.

Unable to stop myself, I step closer. Words leave my lips: "Empress, I can touch you."

"Should I believe that?" She drops her skirt. "If I trusted you, and you lied, I would die."

"Our Lady of Thorns suspects me of lying." I shake my head at the irony. "Not only can I touch you, we were together two games ago."

"Together on a raid? In an alliance? My chronicles say nothing of this."

I gaze past her. "You were separated from your chronicler." After I'd captured the Empress.

"And then?"

"And then we . . . wed."

She laughs. "My Grim Reaper has a sense of humor after all."

I give her a tight nod. "I see I will have to prove it to you."

That night, she wakes with my palm over her mouth. Her eyes flash open.

My bare skin against hers. With Fauna's sentries gone, I easily slipped past the Empress's vines into this villa.

She casts me a murderous look, thinking her life is over.

Seconds tick by. Yet nothing happens. No pain. No streaks of black across her skin. Even though I'd discovered her immunity centuries ago, it still strikes me as miraculous.

Of all the people in the world, over all time, she is the only one I can touch without killing.

She frowns.

"I told you." I remove my hand from her mouth, unable to keep myself from stroking the silken skin of her cheek. So starved for touch.

She blinks at me. "Were we truly married?"

"Yes. Empress, you were born for me, and I for you. One day I will convince you of this."

Brows drawn, she admits, "I've had thoughts of you that I could not reconcile. Desires for you." She runs the pad of her finger over her lips, gaze growing distant.

I swallow thickly. Can she tell how badly I want this to be true? "What are you thinking, Empress?"

She meets my eyes. "Guess."

I answer as honestly as ever. "I believe you plot to take my icon and *all those I've harvested. You wish for them to join your three, and eventually the Priestess's."*

"I would never harm the Priestess; she is my best friend. Fauna was a friend until . . ." She casts me a hurt look. "Why do you think so terribly of me?"

"You killed the Priestess in past games." I've warned the Water Witch, but she swears the Empress is different this time.

"Circe knows this. She has memories from previous games. But I am changed from how I was before." She assesses my face. "I must have hurt you as well."

"You betrayed me."

"How?"

"You tried . . . to kill me on our wedding night." Reminded, I rise, my spurs clinking as I head toward the door.

She sits up, calling, "Where are you going, Reaper?"

Over my shoulder, I say, "To contemplate my next move."

"How long will you be wary of me, my love?" she asks. She is reclining among the pillows on her large bed, sipping wine. Her shift is gauzy, concealing little.

We have been meeting for the last month. She has sent away her disapproving Tarasova, one of many concessions the Empress has made. Slowly this female seduces me to trust her. After my centuries-long solitude, I am helpless not to seek her out. She smiles whenever she first sees me, and excitement lights her glyphs.

Unless it is all a ruse.

She pats the bed beside her. "Will you not sit? Remove your armor, and be comfortable. Have a goblet of wine with me."

I do go to her bed, but I keep my armor on and my sword nearby. Though she is beguiling, I have learned a harsh lesson.

She sits up and reaches for me. Her delicate fingers caress my face. I steel myself, remembering our wedding night, how she sank her claws into my back to inject her poison.

"It is time, Death."

Something in her tone makes my body stir. "Time for what?" She couldn't be speaking of . . .

"For you to claim your wife in truth. I want to be yours. Fully. You've waited centuries; wait no longer."

I know better than to hope, but gods, maybe I could finally know contentment—the kind other men take for granted. I have with me an heirloom wedding ring, have considered giving it to her this night, but I hesitate. "Perhaps I don't yet trust you."

"You know how horrified I am that I hurt you." Her eyes glint. "I would give anything to go back and relive that night."

And I would give anything to know her true thoughts.

"But I can't go back. I can never appease your suspicions." She turns from me. "How can a proud woman offer her body to a male who won't accept it? When he insists on substituting cold metal for warm skin? How can I be with a man who must hate me deep down?"

I lay my hand on her shoulder—the contact is a heady indulgence— but she stiffens at my touch. My brows draw together. I know little of women, have no experience with their ways. But even I know I'm losing her regard.

She's right: if she is different, then I have misjudged her and am unfairly hurting her. "Empress." I cup her cheek. When she faces me again, I say, "Let us start anew with a kiss."

Before I take her lips, she murmurs, "I could love you so easily."

Though I desire her, I do not—and could not—love this creature. Yes, she has been made for me, but perhaps I'm unable to love.

My lips meet hers. My head swims, my senses overloaded. Who needs love when there is this? Contact, warmth, softness, her intoxicating scent. She smells like the meadow flowers that used to bloom near my childhood home.

As I deepen the kiss, I grow drunk on her, on happiness. A future with her spreads out before me. Tonight I will know a woman's flesh, my woman's, and tomorrow we will plan a life together, an existence away from this game.

I take her mouth harder. When she moans for me, the anguish of all those miserable centuries begins to fade.

Over and over I kiss her. Lost in the dizzying sweetness of her lips.

But something needles my mind. Some detail . . .

Roses. Her scent has changed, as it did when she last struck. Pain shoots through my body. Comprehension dawns.

Poison?

She is poisoning me with her lips! Even as I grasp for my sword, part of me is tempted to allow it. To die in her arms. Why live, alone and cursed, forever?

She clutches me harder, wanting the kill. Fury engulfs me, the heat of battle rising. I struggle to draw back, but she has weakened me. In a rage, I shove her away, and my sword flashes out.

Blood arcs across the room.

A flick of my wrist. An instant of action. She is . . . dead.

All my hope dies with her. I had believed her. I had prayed to the gods that this time would be different. That she would at last be mine.

I've waited more than a thousand years for this night—only to be betrayed. I gaze at all the blood. Tonight I have been cursed to several more centuries of waiting for her to return.

"Nooo!" In the next game, I will not be seduced. I will mete vengeance upon her. She will pay for each moment of pain!

The poison lingers. The Empress's sweet taste lingers. I will replay the feel of her lips every night for eternity. I tear apart the room with grief. I tear at my hated armor.

A wave of pain overwhelms me, and I collapse to my knees. She may have delivered enough poison to kill me.

Why live? Why fight?

For retribution. . . .

I've endured all these mind-numbing years just to make her pay. Yet still, I burn for her.

My wife. Maybe I should try one last time.

And maybe you're an idiot, Reaper.

When I'd finally risen on that last fateful night and struggled past the Empress's remains to get to my horse, I'd heard sounds in the cellar. I'd found Circe in chains, drying out, dying of thirst. I'd freed her, then spared her life.

The Priestess had grown suspicious after the Empress had killed Fauna. But before Circe could slip back to the safety of her underwater temple, the Empress had captured her, keeping her alive—so that I wouldn't hear of yet another murder, another betrayal. The treacherous Empress had planned to poison me first, then do away with Circe. . . .

No, I will not be seduced this game. My heart is as black as my armor. The Empress has made it so.

I am Death. When her blood bathes my sword, I will drink it just to mock her.

Unsettled and frustrated, I return the ring to my safe, then cross to the large windows of my study. The sun has set, yet Fauna is heading to the menagerie. She's told me her animals have been behaving strangely. She has no idea what this means, but I do.

The end is nigh. Anticipation is like fire in my veins.

I yank on my gloves and exit the castle. On my way across the grounds, a hot wind gusts over the mountain, and movement above catches my eyes. A strange light appears in the sky, filling me with expectancy.

I can sense deaths coming. Dear gods, I sense a *reckoning* of them.

I pull down my right glove. The rest of the Empress's icon fades before my eyes.

And so it begins. . . .

THE FOOL (0)

Matthew, Gamekeeper of Old

"Crazy like a fox."

A.k.a.: The Hand of Fate, Il Matto, Mat, Null

Powers: Foresight, astral projection, clairaudience, telepathy, dream delivery/scrying/manipulation, memory implantation and absorption, omniscience, and other game-keeping abilities never chronicled.

Special Skills: Genetic memory. Can slow or accelerate the Arcana game. Can call a temporary "trues" (truce).

Weapons: None. If given a weapon, he will toss it away.

Tableau: A smiling young man carries a knapsack and a single white rose. Vacant gaze raised to a blinding sun, he strolls toward the edge of a cliff with a small dog nipping at his heels.

Icon: A null sign: a circle with a diagonal line through it.

Unique Arcana Characteristics: Nose will bleed if he is mentally overloaded from the game.

Before Flash: Living with his mother in the South. Enrolled in a program for autistic students.

HUNTSVILLE, ALABAMA
DAY 0

the Beginning is

darkness

the End   is

two

He hurts

WORSE!

Who is

the hunter   Major Arcana

so strong

Why   will

she   not

listen

Beware   a fox   is as it seems

Foes

hope for hell   terror

Then you'll die

Crazy like a   knight

carry

the memory of

a flower

I'll give

my only friend

another

Matthew

Future flows like

the old

gods

Will we

sleep forever and ever

at

the End

THE MAGICIAN (I)

Finneas, Master of Illusions

"Don't look at this hand, look at that one."

A.k.a.: The Trickster

Powers: Illusion creation and casting. Hallucikinesis, reality distortion, conjurations, and invocations.

Special Skills: Surfing.

Weapons: None.

Tableau: A young man wearing a red robe, holds a wand skyward while pointing to the ground with his free hand. On a table before him lies a pentagram, a chalice, a sword, and a cane. A bed of roses and lilies grow at his feet, vines trailing above.

Icon: Ouroboros.

Unique Arcana Characteristics: Speaks a mysterious magician language when he conjures illusions.

Before Flash: "Problem" kid from California, sent to visit his extended family.

BACKWOODS, NORTH CAROLINA
DAY 0

"I heard you used to live in a mansion in Malibu," the girl said.

What was this chick's name again? I racked my drunken brain. A double-barreled name. Tammy-Something. Uh, what was she doing on the couch with me? She was Buck's girl. "Yeah. I used to."

Until my parents had exiled me.

Only for the summer, they'd said. Finally my time in the woods had been dragging to a close.

Then my folks had enrolled me in school here. *They* had tricked *me.*

Me!

Tonight, I'd guzzled a vat of Natty Light, but this fact wasn't changing. All it'd done was make me more depressed.

Tammy-Something drew her tanned legs up under her, getting comfy. "This must be a big change for you. Going from Cali to the sticks."

When I'd asked my aunt if her grits were non-GMO, she and the rest of the family had laughed till tears streaked down their faces. I told Tammy-Something, "You could say that."

Back home, I'd surfed every morning before school with my best friends. Yet my parents had abandoned me in a place where I had no friends and surfing didn't exist.

No. Freaking. Waves.

It was like my folks *hated* me. Which sucked. Because I missed the hell out of my mom and dad.

And it wasn't as if I could control all this weird shit that kept happening to me. The illusions and hallucinations . . .

Tammy-Something twirled her shiny brown hair. "Is Buck gonna be back anytime soon?"

My oldest cousin was nicknamed Buck—because he'd killed so many deer. Their heads adorned the basement wall; their glassy, accusing eyes were giving me the wiggins.

He had a full gun rack in the back of his souped-up gas guzzler. Weirdly, he and I didn't agree on conserving resources. Or anything at all, for that matter.

"Not likely," I said. He and his two brothers had forced me out into the nearby woods on a mission to go shoot Bambi's mom, and I'd reached my limit. So I'd conjured an illusion of the biggest deer imaginable, the second coming of trophy bucks. They'd set out after it like they were on a quest for freaking fire.

"Guess I'll just wait down here with you." Tammy rose and headed to the fridge, snagging two more beers. She was smoking hot in her tank top and cutoffs—but off-limits.

She returned to the couch, sitting a little too close for comfort. I didn't want Buck to mount *my* stuffed head up on the wall.

She handed me another Natty Light. Had I finished mine? I accepted the can. A little different from the artisanal brand I'd favored in Malibu. "Appreciate it." Was I slurring? The room seemed to tilt.

"How do you like school here?"

I hated Redneck High, home of the Fighting Hicks. Last week, one of my teachers had *winked* as he'd said, "I reckon we can chalk this dry season up to—heh-heh—*global warming*." The cafeteria was neolithic. No gluten-free food. Nothing organic. Not even a juicer.

"It's all right, I guess." My mom had gotten out of this place at eighteen, heading as far away as possible, and she would never return—yet she'd ditched me here.

All because of a few pranks. Maybe she and my dad sensed something was really wrong with me.

When I'd been the only one who could see the illusions, that'd been one thing. But then I'd kinda started using them to jank others. And then I sorta hadn't been able to stop. Even with my folks.

Since their divorce a couple of years ago, they didn't agree on much, yet they'd agreed to cast me out of their lives.

"What are you thinking about?" Tammy-Something asked.

What I usually thought about: "Home."

"A guy like you must have a girlfriend there."

"Nope." Despite my best efforts. I was just the happy-go-lucky buddy type to males and females alike.

She scooted in closer to me, her blue eyes locked on me like I was a target. In a lower tone, she said, "Maybe you could take me for a visit, Finneas. I'd kill to see California."

I swallowed thickly. I was wasted, but I could swear she was putting the moves on me. Natty Light commanded me to kiss her.

I was leaning in when she grabbed my face and put her lips on mine. She had soft lips. They tasted like strawberries and beer. My eyes slid closed when she touched her tongue to mine.

She pulled me in closer, kissing me harder. This chick frenched me like Tongue was an Olympic sport and she was on a medal hunt. I was down. We maneuvered till I was lying on top of her.

In between kisses, she yanked off her shirt, revealing *heaven*.

I rose on straightened arms just to gawk. "Whoa."

With a grin, she pulled a condom from her pocket. This just got better!

Though I always swaggered around like I'd done the deed, I . . . hadn't. Was that about to change at long last?

As I watched in disbelief, she wriggled from her cutoffs and panties.

My eyes widened, my hands fumbling with my fly. We were really about to do this! While she opened the foil pack, I shoved my pants down. She reached for me, and I groaned.

Holy shit, I was in the glide path! *Finally* I was going to get laid.

Nervousness hit me. Would I last long enough? Would I embarrass myself? Natty Light said, "I got you, man." *Think about math, think about the environment. . . .*

What would Buck do if he found out about me and Tammy? Wouldn't matter, I'd be leaving soon.

Then I remembered. No. I wasn't going anywhere. I might be here till I graduated. Would I go two more years without seeing a wave? Had I been completely abandoned?

Stop thinking about that! Tammy wanted to get laid. *I* desperately wanted to get laid—

I might not even get to go home for the holidays.

The thought gutted me. Something like grief wrapped a hand around my throat and squeezed. Ah, God, my eyes were watering! *Finn, you candy-ass punk.*

This close to doing the deed, and I was on the verge of blowing it! *Think about something else; think about* anything *else.*

I sniffled.

Tammy said, "What's the matter?"

"N-nothing."

She sucked in a breath, looking horrified. "What is *wrong* with you, surfer boy? Are you . . . cryin'?"

Humiliation. My face burned as I yanked up my pants. Buck kept telling me I was a weak, weird, pathetic loser.

He was right.

Tammy scrambled for her clothes, shimmying and contorting around me like she was in *The Matrix* and I was contagious.

She was going to tell all her friends what'd happened. *Can't wait for school tomorrow.*

After dressing in record time, she gave me a last look—clearly she now shared Buck's opinion of me—then fled, bounding up the stairs.

Leaving me all alone. Down here in this depressing deer crypt.

I raised another beer to the mounted heads and chugged it. Then this weak, weird, pathetic loser cried himself to sleep. . . .

THE PRIESTESS (II)

Circe Rémire, Ruler of the Deep

"Terror from the abyss!"

A.k.a.: The Water Witch

Powers: Water manipulation, including tidal wave generation and flood creation. Hydrokinetic combat, shapeshifting, and constructs (can form water objects). Hydro scrying (can perceive through water). Hydroportation.

Special Skills: Spells and hexes. One spell enables her to remember past games.

Weapons: Water, trident.

Tableau: A priestess—with water for hair and tentacles for legs—looms over a sacrificial victim at a bloody altar.

Icon: Trident.

Unique Arcana Characteristics: Iridescent blue scales on her arms, with a small fin at each elbow.

Before Flash: A grad student from Bermuda, attending the University of Miami. Her focus: Atlantean mythology and the Bermuda Triangle. Engaged to a computer programmer and instructor there. Member of campus Wiccans.

HAMILTON, BERMUDA
DAY 0

"Are you tipsy?" I asked my soon-to-be husband. I was sitting with my cheek pressed against the door. He was sitting on the other side. It was well past midnight, so we weren't supposed to see each other.

"I might be a tee bit wispy, luv," he said, his voice as jovial as ever. No one had ever made me laugh like Ned. "But my wipsiness can't be helped. My family kept raising their glasses to me. They think I'm a boss for landing a woman as beautiful as you." His crisp British accent got more relaxed when he'd had a drink or two. "My sister said if a movie were made of our lives, it'd be called *The Siren and the Nerd*."

Siren. I frowned as some memory tried to surface. *The ocean's siren song.* . . . I raised my hand to my head as a wave of dizziness overtook me.

Over the last week, the wedding festivities had been going great—until I'd received a long, mysterious wooden box. The accompanying note had been just as puzzling.

Priestess,
Hail Tar Ro. I believe this is yours.
Death

Ever since I'd touched the contents of the package—a golden trident, engraved with cryptic symbols—I'd been having bouts of dizziness, and nightmares about being trapped under the ocean.

I hadn't been able to shake the feeling that something bad was going to happen, as if I was on a countdown clock. And my symptoms were getting worse.

I'd confided them to my grandfather, my best friend. He'd worried that I wasn't ready to marry.

But I am! Ned was the one for me. We were soul mates. I was lucky to have found him.

In a fit two nights ago, I'd taken the trident to a headland cliff and tossed it into the waves. But my issues continued—

"Circe, dear?"

What had he been talking about? Oh, yes . . . "Siren and the Nerd?" I feigned a huff. "They only commented on my looks?"

"They *might* have mentioned your early PhD candidacy, but I told them you were going to cut out all that scholarly rubbish after our nuptials."

I grinned, pressing my palm to the door. I loved this man like a drought loves rain. "My family also spoke a lot about you tonight—about how you went out on the water without your seasickness patch." My brothers had taken him fishing. They'd reported back that they'd never seen anybody throw up so much and live to laugh about it. "*And* without your sunblock." They'd also said they'd never seen anyone burn so fast.

"I did that part on purpose, for my Larry the Lobster impression at the reception. I'm method that way."

Laughter burst from my lips. I'd never known I could laugh this much before Ned. I frowned. No, there'd been another time. . . . In a dark forest, a green-eyed girl and I had laughed till our bellies ached.

"You can't deny the lobster-red hotness of my skin. No, seriously. My skin is literally hot."

I tsked. "And you'll be bright red for all our photos tomorrow."

"We can always hope I'll be *peeling* by then." Ned sighed. "How you put up with me is a mystery."

A voice in my head murmured, *Mysteries from the deep.* The nightmares. *Shake it off, Circe.*

"You're brave to want kids with me, luv. Three no less."

I'd told him I wanted to get started once I'd earned my degree. He'd saluted me, replying, "I shall enthusiastically contribute to this endeavor. You will know what the word *commitment* means."

Now he asked, "What if they turn out to be nerds who get seasick?"

"Then you'll know you're the father."

He laughed. "You give as good as you get. God, I'm ready to get this wedding business sorted, so we can get back to *us*."

"I know. I feel as if I haven't seen you in weeks."

"I don't like sleeping in different beds. Custom or not, if you have another nightmare, you need to come get me."

"I will," I lied. I'd had several each night since that package's arrival. Yet those nightmares had felt more like . . . memories. Maybe I was losing my mind. "You know how much I love you, right?"

"Ah, but the merest fraction of how much I love you."

"I'm serious, Ned." I could all but *hear* him frowning. I glanced at my arm. For an instant, my skin appeared to glitter. Like a fish's scales. "I knew the night we met that you would be mine." I'd been giving a campus lecture on the Bermuda Triangle and Atlantean folklore, presenting pictures of Circe's Abyss, the deepest spot in the Triangle.

The abyss I'd been named after.

A deep-water oceanography team had recently completed the imaging of it. Those images had captured an underground aquifer—*below* the abyss.

And inside the aquifer was a rock formation so exact that it had to be man-made.

If the formation was a structure from a sunken city—such as Atlantis—how had it gotten into an aquifer?

Like a ship in a bottle. . . .

Though Ned, a brilliant computer programmer, was devoted to hard science, for some reason he'd attended my lecture. He'd grasped anything I could throw his way, asking observant questions. He hadn't scoffed when I'd told him of my Wiccan leanings.

Afterward, coffee had turned to drinks. Drinks to dinner. Since then, we'd never separated a single night. Until now. "I thought you were adorable," I said. "Your cheeks flushed whenever I looked at you."

"Because I kept saying to myself, *I think I'm bloody in love with her.* I didn't know how it could be possible, but there it was."

I murmured, "There it was." I imagined his palm pressed against the door, opposite mine.

Strange how the wood burl beneath my hand looked like a whirlpool. I shivered. Clearing my throat, I asked, "Will you finally admit why you came to my lecture?" He'd teased me with different reasons: Because he'd ducked in out of the rain (it'd been clear that day). To sample the free lukewarm coffee. To kill time until his superhero gig started.

"The truth? What would you say if I told you a mate made me a wager?"

I made my tone scandalized. "A *wager?* What were the terms?"

"He bet me a hundred quid that the woman hosting this Atlantean lecture would be the most beautiful creature on earth." He exhaled. "Best hundred I ever lost."

I squeezed my eyes closed. "Everyone calls you a comedian, but I think you're really a romantic."

"God, I'm going to enjoy teasing *and* romancing you for the next eighty or so years of our lives."

"Do you really think we'll live that long?" That wood burl on the door appeared to spin.

"Of course. Laughter and love keep a body young."

I inhaled a deep breath. My big day had finally come. *I can do this.*

I'd sent everyone in the bridal party away, needing time to compose myself before the sunset ceremony. In the few hours I'd dozed after talking to Ned, the nightmares/memories had come on full-bore. All morning and afternoon, I'd battled anxiety. Again, I sensed a countdown ticking.

Toward what?

I shook my head hard. I just needed to get down the aisle and reach Ned. He would make me feel better. His eyes would light up when he saw me in this gorgeous strapless dress. I would muffle a laugh when I saw the tips of his ears and his nose peeling.

Bouquet in hand, I took a step.

In the wrong direction. Left was toward the chapel ceremony; right would take me to the beach. Another step to the right.

I strained every muscle to get to Ned, but my feet wouldn't obey me. *I'm losing my mind, losing my mind!* My eyes went wide when I opened the door and headed outside—away from the chapel—from the man I loved.

I wanted to call for him; no sounds would pass my lips. When I reached the pink-sand beach, the sunset gleamed over the placid water. My arms fell limp by my sides, my bouquet dropping soundlessly in the sand.

Tears of frustration welled. What force had taken me over? Would Ned think I'd run away? That I didn't want to marry him?

I struggled to scream, "I love you!" Yet couldn't speak at all.

The sea had always called to me, but now . . . now its siren song was undeniable. Suddenly, I knew where I was going. Toward that abyss.

I had *always* been headed toward the abyss.

Tears streamed down my face. *Ned will think I left him.* I reached the water, and the gentle waves lapped at my ankles. A glimmer beneath the surf caught my eye.

Somehow the trident had returned to me.

As I dipped to collect it, a tingling sensation flowed up my forearms, and light-blue scales appeared there, like long, iridescent gloves. They sparkled in the sunlight. My elbows itched maddeningly. I scratched them, and my skin sloughed off—to make way for jutting blue fins.

I sobbed. How could Ned ever want me like this?

Those cryptic symbols on my trident were now legible to me. They read: *The Abysmal Ruler of the Deep.*

In a daze, I cradled the weighty gold weapon in my arms and waded into the water up to my knees. To my waist. To my neck. I did not stop until I was submerged.

I expelled my last breath, awaiting the burning suffocation of water filling my lungs, but instead I . . . *became* the sea.

The weight of my trident made me sink. The pressure didn't bother me. The temperature had no effect. I could see, hear, feel, taste, even scent through the water. This jumble of new sensations made me giddy, as if my soul was soaring—instead of sinking.

Deeper and deeper I dropped. Although it should have been pitch black as the waning daylight faded above me, somehow I could see. Luminescent sharks darted through me. Plankton and crustaceans tumbled within me as if buffeted by an island breeze.

I descended till I'd reached the bottom of Circe's Abyss. Rocks parted, revealing a vortex that led beneath the seafloor shelf. To the aquifer?

I was swept into the vortex, then sucked even lower through a tunnel—as if down a drain. Or down Alice's rabbit hole.

The water turned fresh. Before me was the structure from those pictures! I flowed around the stone exterior.

Swarms of phosphorescent creatures teemed on the walls, illuminating carvings in the rock. The symbols were from the same language as the words engraved on my trident. I read:

Abysmal temple of the Great Priestess, the Ruler of the Deep.
All who hear the Priestess's call will fear her catastrophal powers.
TERROR FROM THE ABYSS.

This structure, these markings, those creatures . . . I was seeing things no normal human had ever beheld. All my life, I'd been obsessed with the sea, with Atlantis.

I *was* the sea. Was I also an Atlantean?

Live coral adorned an entrance, each branch ending in a trident shape.

Curiosity driving me, I flowed through the opening. Inside was an airlock with steps rising out of the water. I instinctively knew how to regrow my form, to become a woman again. Trident in hand, I arose from the sea and climbed the steps.

Shafts of that phosphorescent light beamed inside. Shadows rippled.

Ancient mosaics decorated the walls. I ran my fingertips over the damp tiles. The eerie scenes depicted tidal waves engulfing helpless lands, and monstrous sea life—giant sharks, whales, squids, a kraken—attacking ships. The shadows made the scenes appear to move.

Chills skittered up my back when I came upon a bloodstained altar, liberally carved with trident symbols. I glanced at my own weapon.

Could this be *my* temple? Hadn't Death called me "Priestess"?

As I eased farther inside, memories from my dreams arose. This place *was* mine.

I got the sense that my temple was a refuge. But also a . . . jail? Somehow I knew I would quickly die on land, but *slowly* die here in this lonely, echoing abyss.

Solitude would be my punishment, and fear my jailor. What crime had I committed to be cursed like this?

No, I didn't care about my fate; one way or another I would return to Ned! He would accept these changes in me. I believed in him.

I ran to the airlock and became the sea once more. I'd almost reached the top of the tunnel when the seafloor above began to quake.

The water was heating. I gazed up from the tunnel opening, disbelieving my vision.

A giant submarine was hurtling down, far too fast to be a normal descent through the depths.

Past the vessel, I could see lights in the sky—as if the ocean above me had disappeared, the water sucked out.

Though it must be night, the sun seemed to be shining. And I thought I saw a sky full of . . . flames. I was riveted. Until that light went dark—snuffed by the submarine crashing down atop my only exit.

I was trapped.

In my lonely, echoing abyss.

THE EMPEROR (IV)

Richter, Stone Overlord

"Quake before me!"

A.k.a.: Jersey Number Four

Powers: Pyromancy, magma generation, terramancy. Can create and control fire, mountains, volcanoes, and earthquakes.

Special Skills: Athletic skill, brute strength.

Weapons: Rock and fire.

Tableau: A stony-eyed ruler, surrounded by flames and slabs of granite, holding a scepter with an engraved ankh.

Icon: Ankh.

Unique Arcana Characteristics: Lava flows from his bleeding hands, and his eyes glow like fire.

Before Flash: Right wing for Oshawa Generals, Ontario Junior Hockey League team, NHL hopeful.

VANCOUVER, BRITISH COLUMBIA
DAY O

I hope I broke Number Eight's fucking neck. I kicked back in the penalty box—the sin bin—as they loaded him onto a stretcher.

Minutes ago, I'd body-checked the shit out of Eight, and our sticks had "accidentally" crossed. Now he was moaning on his side, dribbling teeth onto the ice like they were Chiclets.

I didn't enforce just for a game. I enforced *for life.*

Scouts loved that shit; they were on their phones in the stands now.

I'd earned my nickname of Richter—because I put players into the boards with the force of an earthquake. Good thing, too. How else was I gonna show the scouts what I was capable of? Fight? Whenever I tore off my gloves and yelled, "You wanna go?" more and more players skated away. Eight was from the States, must not have heard to steer clear of me. Most of the others had. Hell, I thought I'd even dated Twenty's sister.

Yeah, I remembered now. She was a crier.

I glanced at my older brother. Brody was at the edge of the rink, leaning heavily on his cane. He was still a badass, even though he couldn't skate anymore, could barely walk.

Because of me.

At fourteen, I'd gotten hauled in for questioning (the bitch thought she could "change her mind" after teasing me all night?), and he'd come to bail me out. On the way home—*wham!*

Car crash.

In seconds, he'd gone from star player to cripple. Then later to my agent and coach. Weeks after the accident, he'd told me, "You're quick, you're still growing, and you're mean. By the time I'm done with you,

you'll fly over the ice. You'll be big as a tank. Nobody'll be more vicious. The perfect grinder."

His coaching technique? Pain. Lots of it. Every time I fucked up.

At first I was so slow and stupid he had to use his cane on me every day. Now only a couple of times a week. . . .

Number Eight didn't move as they wheeled his stretcher away, didn't even give a feeble wave to the crowd so they could cheer.

I shared a look with Brody, not quite a smile. His beefy face was just like mine, a face that turned ugly when he smiled. He'd noticed the scouts' interest too. It was all happening according to his plan: Red Wings before I turned eighteen, then Stanley Cup by twenty.

I mouthed to him, *I told you so.* He'd been thinking those new accusations would follow me to Vancouver, had been worrying for no reason.

Nothing could touch me!

I glanced at the game clock, and got a spike of adrenaline. Three . . . two . . . one . . .

Back on the ice. Puck in play.

Number Twenty was giving me looks like he wanted to dance. At the thought, my body got hot, my skin flushed. This was what I loved! He was coming right at me. *Bring it on, you little bitch!*

Out of the corner of my eye, I saw Number Thirty too late. Double-teaming me—

WHAM. As hard as the car wreck . . .

Next time I opened my eyes, I saw the roof of the stadium. Couldn't breathe! I was laid out on the ice, gliding across the surface like a puck. Needed air! I was *never* on the ice.

They were laughing. Twenty skated closer, skidding inches from my head to spray my face with ice shavings. "That's for my sister, you sick fuck."

I needed to pummel their faces to meat! To goddamn meat! *Breathe, Richter!* Why couldn't I move? My vision was going blurry, my body fever-hot. My fists felt like they were burning!

I got the weird sensation that I was sinking. Was the rink . . . *melting*? Surely I was unconscious, and this was a dream.

People started screaming. Players tried to run/skate off the thawing rink. There was no more smooth ice, just slush and sand. My head lolled to one side, and I saw my right hand. The glove looked like goop, like soup spilled on my knuckles. Melted too? Impossible.

Suddenly light flared through the stadium roof; outside the night was . . . day? Was I dying? Going to the light? I'd dreamed of hellfire for so long, there was no way I was going *up*.

More screams. That meant everyone else was seeing this! Where was Brody?

Fire rained down, flames landing all around me, *on* me. They didn't burn. Felt . . . *good*. My lids went heavy.

No! I had to get up. I needed to get to my brother! I struggled to rise. The world seemed to tilt.

My eyes rolled back in my head, and my mind went under. . . .

When I came to, I couldn't see shit. How long had I been out? I rubbed my eyes. Wait, where were my helmet and gloves? My pads and jersey? I slowly sat up. As my vision cleared, I saw black char marks all over my buck-naked body, but no burns. I gazed around. My brain refused to compute this sight.

The stadium was gone; only the metal skeleton that used to be the bleachers and a ring of steel girders were left. Farther out was a parking lot full of scorched cars. Tires smoked.

All around me were weird piles of ash. I made it to my bare feet. Where the hell were my skates? I blinked down at a pair of blades. My skates had . . . burned away.

Where the hell was Brody???

I lumbered toward the bleachers. I was sore, the way I got if I didn't practice for a couple of days. Damn it, how long had I been out?

I passed an ash pile. Skate blades jutted from the bottom. Was that . . . a player? I saw another pile, and another, all with blades. Somehow their bodies had burned to ash. We must've been bombed by terrorists or something!

How had I survived? Why had I *liked* the fires hitting me?

"Brody!" I yelled. Silence.

I ran toward the spot where he'd been standing, hoping to see footprints in the ash. Instead, I found the golden end of his wooden cane, as well as the surgical implant they'd put in his knee. I shuffled the ash, uncovering the titanium rod that had been attached to his spine.

This is my brother. Brody was dead.

Rage like I'd never known exploded inside me, the need to *kill*—

The ground ruptured between my feet. I yelled, lunging to one side. When the crevice yawned wider, I took off in a sprint toward the parking lot, running full speed between scorched cars. But the opening kept growing, the edge right at my goddamned heels, like it was chasing me! Cars toppled down; ash swirled in the air till I could barely see, barely breathe.

It'll catch me, then I'll fall straight to hell!

The pavement disappeared beneath me. I lurched in midair and latched onto the side of the crevice, digging my fingers into the crumbling asphalt.

Choking on ash. Heart thundering. Legs flailing to find a foothold.

As I scrambled for a better grip, I glanced over my shoulder. The rift went so far down I'd never stop falling. Just go on forever.

A gust of steam shot up, wetting my skin. My fingers started to give way. *Hold on, Richter! Hold on, you bitch-ass!*

One finger slipped . . . two more . . . One hand.

'Bout to die. A yell ripped from my lungs. I was dangling from three fingers when another gust hit me from below.

Game over—

I dropped.

Inches? What the?? I frowned down at my feet. My body was . . . rising?

All around me *lava* bubbled up, wrapping me like a soft blanket.

It didn't burn. No, the lava just carried me along.

Like a gift from hell. . . .

THE HIEROPHANT (V)

Guthrie, He of the Dark Rites

"We go now to our bloody business."

A.k.a.: The Sacrificer, the Consecrator

Powers: Mind control, mesmerism, pathokinesis (emotion manipulation).

Special Skills: Genetic memory. Has an innate knowledge of sacrificial rituals. His mind control can last even after he's dead.

Weapons: His brainwashed followers.

Tableau: A robed male holding his right hand high, two fingers raised, blessing his white-eyed followers.

Icon: Two raised fingers.

Unique Arcana Characteristics: Pale from cannibalistic diet. Teeth filed into sharp points. Eyes turn white when he uses his mind-control power.

Before Flash: Miner.

THE LOVERS (VI)

Vincent and Violet, Duke and Duchess Most Perverse

"We will love you. In our own way."

A.k.a.: The Milovníci twins.

Powers: Pathokinesis and love manipulation (can warp and pervert any who love). Replication (can create *carnates*, living duplicates of themselves). Command inducement and sense scrying (can command carnates and borrow their senses).

Special Skills: Torture.

Weapons: Their carnates. Also, torture implements, pistols, booby-traps, explosives.

Tableau: Look-alike twins, a male and a female, stand hand in hand with a bloody windmill spinning in the background and dead roses at their feet.

Icon: Two overlapping triangles, bisected with arrows.

Unique Arcana Characteristics: Violet is part of Vincent, an absorbed twin.

Before Flash: Lived their entire lives in the Shrine, their father's doomsday bunker, studying their line's chronicles.

THE CENTURION (VII)

Kentarch Mgaya, Wicked Champion

"Woe to the bloody vanquished."

A.k.a.: The Chariot, the Wanderer, the Phantom

Powers: Teleportation. Ghosting (intangibility, can phase rapidly between corporeal and incorporeal.). Ghosting extension (can make objects and other people intangible). Superior aiming.

Special Skills: Covert operations, intelligence collection, tactical satellite communications, target acquisition, and offensive raiding. Marksmanship.

Weapons: Whatever's available.

Tableau: A warrior in a horse-drawn chariot, dressed in a red tunic and a helmet with a red-feather crest. Waterfalls and waves appear in the background.

Icon: Horse's head.

Unique Arcana Characteristics: When intangible, a faint outline of his body remains.

Before Flash: Newlywed Kenya Special Forces soldier, training an elite anti-poaching unit. Descended from a long line of Maasai warriors.

IN THE SHADOW Of MOUNT KENYA
DAY O

Outnumbered and outgunned.

At least a dozen poachers fired on me with automatic rifles, their bullets chewing up the side of my truck. On the other side, I hunched down, taking cover, my own rifle in hand.

I'd already used most of my ammo, was down to my last four bullets. Sweat dripped into my eyes as I awaited an opportunity to return fire.

To think I'd once complained that my new assignment here would be too soft! When my superiors had dispatched me to this park to train rangers, I'd wondered why they would punish me.

I wasn't simply a soldier in the KSF; I was the best, breaking records so thoroughly they would stand forever. I'd learned from my father, an unmatched lion hunter, that there was power in excellence.

Then I'd quickly discovered that a conservation ranger's job was not only dangerous—it was a widow-maker. Every animal was a target of poachers, but especially the rhinos, with horns worth more than their weight in gold. This park had become a frenzied war zone.

Though my wife had been afraid a lion would get me, a far more dangerous predator had me in its sights.

One shot rang out above the others, echoing over the plain. It blasted straight through my truck, inches from my head. A high-caliber hunting rifle. Gasoline began to pour from a hole in the tank.

The gunfire ebbed. "You don't belong here, soldier!" one of the poachers yelled. "You never should have come!"

They wanted revenge for the deaths of their men during an earlier shootout with my conservation rangers. Today this gang had caught me driving alone to retrieve gear I'd used for a drill, my last task before my leave began.

"Surrender, and you'll live," another one shouted. "Stay and die. This is your last chance to walk away."

A lie. They executed anyone who laid down arms.

But surrender still beckoned. My beautiful Issa was expecting me home tonight. My yearning to get back to her played tricks on my mind, whispering, "These men are telling the truth. Of course they will let you go home."

I forced myself to accept reality. I would die if I fought; I would die if I didn't.

I am already dead.

I replayed Issa tracing the claw-mark scars across my chest, asking me not to take this park assignment because of the lions. I'd explained to her that I had *earned* those scars. I'd heard the maddened lion roaring with fury, warning me away, and still I'd foolishly stalked it.

I'd vowed to her that I would be safe because I would never ignore a warning again.

Yet now I was a dead man. Hatred for these poachers blistered me inside. I could at least take a few of them with me. "No surrender!" I leapt up, pivoting and aiming through the busted windows of my truck. Two controlled shots. I hit one poacher between the eyes. Another in the skull. I dropped back down. "Not today!"

They opened up with their machine guns, spraying bullets.

Amid the gunfire, I caught a different sound—a copter? Coming up from behind the ridge? If it was the park's copter, I might live. If it was theirs, I would die.

A lull. I chanced another shot, hitting my third target. One bullet left.

The helicopter appeared over the rise. . . .

Not ours. Two shooters inside had me dead to rights.

A dying man's life truly did flash before him. Mine had been filled with polarities and extremes. Fundamental forces in combat.

Old and new. Life and death. Love and hate.

Ancient Maasai tradition clashed with my modern military life. I'd hunted lions as a boy; now I protected them.

I delivered death to so many men—three this day alone—but Issa and I were trying for a baby.

My love for her left me reeling sometimes. But so did my hatred for my enemies.

Beyond the helicopter, Mount Kenya stood proud. My family had lived, warred, loved, and died on these plains for centuries. Sun struck the peak.

My instinct was to close my eyes. But I refused. I straightened my beret and prayed to my spirit guardian. Maybe my ancestors were wrong; maybe there was an afterlife.

I rose with my rifle in my outstretched hand—the posture of surrender. I stared them down, standing as proud as the mountain. But I'd be as unpredictable as a lion. I jerked my rifle to my shoulder and fired my last bullet, hitting the pilot—

Gunshots erupted from the copter.

I felt no pain. Had I died? Dozens of bullets had passed through my body. Suddenly I felt weightless—I must be leaving this world.

I only wished I could have seen Issa one last time.

As the copter plummeted into the ridge, I did shut my eyes, closing the cover on the book of my life.

I waited.

And waited.

When I opened my eyes, I stood in the bedroom of our little apartment in Nairobi. Was I already a ghost? Issa strolled out of the steamy bathroom, wrapped in a towel. Her face lit up into a smile.

She could see me?

In a delighted tone, she said, "You're early! I wanted everything to be ready when you got here. The apartment was supposed to smell like nyama choma and biryani, and I would look like a pinup. *Sawa sawa.*" No worries. "I will take this surprise any day." She hurried to give me an embrace. "Ooh, you smell like gasoline." But she didn't release me.

I still hadn't spoken, hadn't moved. I must be alive. Maybe I'd had a mental breakdown.

She drew back. *"Hujambo?"* Everything okay?

I finally found my voice. *"Sijambo."* I'm fine. I pulled my beret off. My throat was tight as I said, "I am very glad to see you, Issa."

Later that evening, we lay in bed, sharing a warm bottle of Tusker's.

What if this night with Issa was all a dream? If I fell asleep, it might come to an end.

The thought chilled me. I decided to remain awake as long as possible, to spend as much time with her as I could.

She had curled up against me, was again tracing the scars across my chest. The skin that should be riddled with bullet holes.

All night I'd been replaying the shootout. Those bullets had passed through me as if I'd already been a spirit.

"Don't go back," Issa said with a pensive look on her beautiful face.

Don't punish my enemies? "Let us talk tomorrow." Today had been strange enough. After returning home from the madness of the park, I'd received a bizarre package: a satellite phone with one preprogrammed number, sealed in a military-grade storage case. I'd seen these in my training. The case would withstand fire, water, even an electronic pulse.

Reading the accompanying note had brought on a wave of dizziness:

Centurion,
When the end begins, contact me.
Death

Why would a man named Death call me "Centurion"? His note had called to mind a tale I'd learned as a young *moran*. Among the Maasai, the *morani*, warriors, were distinct from the *laiboni*, spiritual guides and healers, but one legendary man had been both.

Kentarch of the Legion.

The namesake of every firstborn male in my line, he was said to have rescued a lost Roman legion from starvation, becoming a blood brother to a centurion.

Kentarch had been a killer and a healer, filled with polarities, just like me. He'd also possessed unique gifts, had been able to vanish into thin air and reappear on the other side of the Great Rift Valley.

Fearing his power, other tribes had tried to kill him, attacking with their *marungu*. But none of those throwing clubs struck him. In front of all his people, he'd become a ghost.

Had I inherited the first Kentarch's powers? Perhaps I could become a ghost at will. The poachers would stand no chance. . . .

I gazed up with a frown when a hot breeze blew in through the open windows, rustling the curtains. Nights were usually cool here this time of year.

Issa said, "So warm?"

Shouts sounded outside. I rose and crossed to the balcony to investigate. The sky grew brighter before my eyes. Fantastical lights began to gleam on the horizon.

What wonder was this? "Issa, come. You must see." I stared up in awe.

She joined me at the balcony rail, and we watched the spectacle together. She whispered, *"Ajabu."* Amazing.

Through sheer will, I forced my gaze away from the sky. Though I longed to look at those lights, my wife was the wonder of my life. I would much rather look at her, and I might be on borrowed time with her.

A thunderous sound rolled in the night. When it increased in intensity, my blood grew cold. "Did you hear that?" I didn't know what was creating that sound, but I understood the message.

"Hmm?" Issa murmured without a care as the lights danced in her eyes.

The sound was the warning roar—of every lion that had ever lived. . . .

Strength (VIII)

Lark Inukai, Mistress of Fauna

"Red of tooth and claw!"

A.k.a.: Fortitude

Powers: Animal manipulation (can control all creatures). Animal scrying (can borrow the senses of animals). Animal generation (her blood affects the physiology of creatures and can make them into her familiars). Enhanced senses, night vision.

Special Skills: Healing and training animals.

Weapons: Beastly predators.

Tableau: A delicate girl in a white robe controlling the gaping jaws of a lion.

Icon: Paw print.

Unique Arcana Characteristics: Has claws and fangs. Her eyes turn red when she mingles her senses with a creature's.

Before Flash: High school student and animal trainer, living on the compound of an eccentric billionaire.

CRAZYCAKES' CRIB
DAY 0

"I'm dead meat," I muttered when I smelled blood in the boss's menagerie. "Just kill me now." The animals were going nuts!

They'd been acting weird for days, but now they chewed at their enclosures, head-butted the walls of their pens, and dug in a frenzy. Even passive animals fought.

Rabbits in a death match. What the hell?

If they kept this up, we were going to lose stock. Probably had already. The smell of blood made me light-headed.

I yanked my phone out of my jeans pocket and called my dad. His line rang. And rang. Voice mail.

I frowned. He *always* picked up, because he knew how freaked out I would get if he didn't.

Four years ago, Mom had deserted us. My first clue? She hadn't answered when I'd called for a ride home from school. She'd *never* answered.

I left a message for my dad: "The animals are freaking out for some reason. We've got mass injuries, and I need your help. Please come home. Love you." I texted: HELP! Animals injured. Where r u?

The menagerie was as big as an arena, housing hundreds of creatures. How to calm them all down? I spun in circles. I needed one-on-one time to work my magic. Not one-on-hundreds!

I could medicate some, hose others, but I'd never get to the majority in time.

More blood, more growls, more damage. I spun faster, yelling, *"EVERYBODY CHILL THE HELL OUT!"*

Quiet. I stilled, gazing around. Animals stared at me from all sides with wide eyes, motionless.

Damn, I was *good.*

Time to triage this crisis. I popped a crick in my neck on the way to the nearest line of pens. I did spot assessments, but found injuries everywhere.

Maybe the boss wouldn't notice we were light a few dozen animals. As I combed through the enclosures along the north side, I swallowed with fear at the thought of explaining this to Mr. Deth. He wasn't cruel or anything, just really intimidating.

Partly because he was rich as all get out (like, Richie Rich), even though he was only in his early twenties.

Partly because he was drop-dead gorgeous. I mean, absolutely to-die-for with his light blond hair, tanned face, and vivid amber eyes.

And partly because he was crazy. . . .

No fatal wounds on the north side! I hurried down the west one. We'd lost one of three bandicoots, and a roo had a broken tail—

I stopped dead in my tracks. The cougars had chewed their cage open! Those four were like freaking velociraptors! Only not as friendly.

So where were they?

I heard a snarl on the south wall of pens and ran like a bat out of hell. "Shit, shit!" I skidded to a halt in front of the wolf habitat.

The two adults had been shredded, their bodies lifeless in the sawdust. They'd died to protect their pups.

The cougars had cornered the three. The pups cowered, whimpering, blood all over them. Ah, God, the little runt was missing an eye.

One cougar had its paw raised for a killing blow.

I didn't think; I ran into the middle of the clash. The cougar swiped my leg, snarling its fury.

"Oh, you dick! Get out!"

The four swished their tails. They clearly had no intention of giving up their prey. I swallowed with fear.

Then I remembered: I was Lark Inukai. I defanged killers. I found their weaknesses and exploited them ruthlessly.

I focused on the sole female, staring her down. To the males, it'd look like I'd singled her out for attack. I drew my lips back from my teeth, and growled at her.

The three males blinked, tails going still. They wouldn't want to lose their only babe.

"OUT! NOW!"

They jolted, spinning in midair to beeline back to their cage. "That's right, assholes!"

Exhaling a breath, I knelt beside the pups. Their own blood matted their fur. They needed a vet to patch them up. *Call me, Dad!*

"Come here, little guys." I examined them as best as I could, assessing their wounds. I thought they would live, but muscles had been severed, their skin slashed open. One's face was clawed up. The runt would be half-blind. "Guess I'll call you Cyclops, huh?"

My own eyes watered, and I tumbled back on my ass. Two wolves dead on my watch, and three pups injured. The pack had been decimated. Not to mention all the other animals.

The pups licked my bleeding wound, their way of showing care. "I appreciate the gesture, little guys, but I'll be okay. Come on, let's get you out of here." I wanted them away from their dead sire and dam.

I picked up the three and headed toward an empty pen. "Here we go." I gently set them down, then locked them in, steeling myself when they whimpered in panic. "I've gotta check on everybody. I'll be back soon."

I hurried past the fourth wall of enclosures. We'd lost more animals, but every other injury could keep for now.

The wolves would get priority. I would clean their wounds and administer a sedative/painkiller. As I headed to the supply room, I pulled my phone out, trying Dad again.

He was going to be so disappointed by all this. He made a habit of underpromising and overdelivering with the boss.

Still no answer? Panic bubbled up. No, no, Dad was just out of a service area. Between towers.

Calm yo tits, Lark. He would never abandon me.

I shoved my phone back into my pocket. Tonight was going to be a long one.

Damn it, how had *I* ended up in this situation? I'd barely believed it when Dad had sold his practice and taken this job. Granted, his ginormous salary wasn't exactly chicken feed, but I'd had a life: school, friends, my training business. I'd had to give up everything because of Mr. Deth.

Dad genuinely liked the dude. He'd told me he'd never met a smarter—or lonelier—man.

I could see both. The boss had never had a visitor out to this isolated compound. The only calls he got were about supply shipments. If his phone rang, he never glanced down at a number and smiled as he answered. In fact, I'd never seen him smile at all.

His solitude had confused me. He was rich and hot, tall with a great body, and he had this really cool accent. Latvian or something. Which explained the weird-ass last name.

I'd told him once, "Your name sounds like *death*, as in *dying*."

His face had been completely expressionless as he'd said, "Does it, then?"

I'd wondered why he was alone—until he'd hinted that the Big One was coming. He was fortifying his mountain compound for some catastrophe.

Everything had begun to make sense. *He's a crazycakes prepper.* His insanity had kept him from finding friends or a girlfriend. He probably had a germ phobia too; dude wore gloves at all times.

I turned the corner—and almost ran into him. My breath strangling in my throat, I craned my head up to meet his gaze. "You scared me!" I was as nervous as a cat on hot bricks. "Uh, what's shaking, Boss?"

"We must return to the castle. A storm is coming."

Weird. "I'll be there in a sec. There's been a little, uh, situation"—*bloodbath*—"with the animals." How was I going to worm my way out of this?

"Yes, I scent the blood and death. But that doesn't matter. We return. *Now.*" He grabbed my elbow, startling me.

"Um, the cougars aren't totally secured. And there're some injuries that need tending." My little wolves . . .

"Later." He steered me toward the exit.

Outside, a hot wind blew, so different from the cool breezes we normally got up here. Then I nearly stumbled. The sky was alight with gorgeous streams of color. Even the boss paused, staring up at the sight.

My concern for the animals faded as I lost myself in those lights. I murmured, "God, they're so beautiful."

"Beautiful?" He started dragging me to the castle. "Remember: *beautiful* means we must turn away."

But I couldn't! I never wanted to turn away. "I need to look at them a little while longer. Please, Boss!"

He forced me inside. I was tempted to slip past him for another peek, but he pressed some buttons on a wall keypad.

Whirring sounded all around us. It took a moment to register—he was closing the shutters over the windows and the doors! How would I get out? "Why are you battening down? I have to go check on the animals as soon as possible."

"The menagerie will be protected against whatever approaches."

The little hairs on my nape rose. "What's approaching?"

"A catastrophe."

Crazycakes! "Like the Big One?" My situation grew brutally clear. I was trapped in a mountaintop fortress with a madman. "Uh, I really need to get in touch with my dad."

"Be my guest." He waved one gloved hand. "Tell him to turn away from the light and seek immediate shelter."

I yanked out my phone, hitting redial. *Pick up, Dad, please pick up!* Voice mail. Dialed him again.

I'd just stowed my phone when my vision dimmed—and dimmed some more—until I couldn't see at all. "Oh, God, what's happening??" I blinked over and over. Suddenly, I could see again *from within the menagerie.* I cried, "What is going on?" Across the central pen, I caught sight of the pups. The three were growing before my eyes, their wounds healing over and scarring.

They were *massive*, bigger than any wolf I'd ever seen. "I-I think I'm going crazy!"

"Fauna, stay calm," Boss said. "This is to be expected."

I blinked. Hard. And again. As quickly as my vision had gone wonky, it was restored. I stared at Mr. Deth. "Who the hell is Fauna?"

"You melded your senses with one of your creatures. You saw through the eyes of an animal."

"A) What are you talking about? And, B) What I saw can't be happening."

"What did you see?"

"The wolf pups were growing. They were . . . huge."

He glanced down at my injured leg. "Did they happen to taste your blood?"

I nodded.

He raised a brow. "That was unexpected. Yes, the trio will become *quite* large."

"Why? What does this have to do with my blood?"

"Come with me," he said, heading to the security room. I hesitantly followed. "Sit." He pointed to a chair in front of the camera feeds from around the castle.

I perched on the edge of the seat. "You've gotta tell me what's going on 'cause I'm about to freak out."

With his gaze on the screens, he said, "The trump cards of a Tarot deck—the Major Arcana—are real. You are Strength. Also known as Fauna."

Why did that sound so . . . right?

"I am the Death Card."

"Like y-your last name? Deth?"

He shook his head. "Like the Grim Reaper."

A low roar buzzed in my ears. He sounded so far away as he continued his wackadoodle explanation:

". . . twenty-two players in a lethal game . . . reincarnated every few centuries . . . special powers individual to each card . . . out to smite one another . . . deadly killers with but one aim."

He must be mad as a March hare, with bats in the belfry. Yet I felt as if puzzle pieces were clicking into place.

" . . . give me loyalty, and I will teach you much about the game, as if your own family had chronicled. And I will let you live longer than the others."

"Whoa." *Let* me live? "Are you saying . . . does that mean you're gonna *kill* me?" What a stupid question; how many murderers would ever admit that?

In his deep, accented voice, he told me, "Yes, Fauna. In time, I will take your life." He was calmly telling me he'd gank me. "You might have a couple of years left before then. Perhaps you'll make it out of your teens. I haven't decided yet."

He sounded so confident that I nearly puked with fear.

The roar grew louder. Not just in my ears?

Death fell silent, cocking his head. "It begins at the end. The reckoning comes."

"My dad is out there!"

"Yes."

An explosion of brightness lit up the screens; the castle rocked. The cameras cut out, leaving only static.

I was curled up and crying in my bed, terrified for Dad—and for myself. Some catastrophe was happening out there, which meant Death had been right all along about the Big One.

I believed him about the game. I believed he would kill other kids one by one until he finally got to me.

I believed I might never see my dad's patient smile again. Had I lost *both* of my parents? Though I hated my mom, I didn't want her to die. In these terrifying hours, I'd even tried her old number. Not that any of my calls had connected.

Dad, please be safe. Please come back. Some crazy dude wants to murder me.

How could this be happening? What if Dad made it back, but Death had already ganked me? I buried my face in my pillow to muffle my scream. Then I remembered something.

I was Lark freaking Inukai. I sat up, swiping my tears away. I defanged killers. I defused their aggression. I found out their weaknesses and exploited them ruthlessly.

You don't know me, Death.

Every dangerous creature had a weakness. I would find his. If we were supposed to play to win, I would dominate.

You don't know me at all. . . .

THE HERMIT (IX)

Arthur, Master of Alchemy

"A wise man in the guise of a boy."

A.k.a.: The Alchemist

Powers: Hyperintelligence, hypercognition, chemistry savant, guile. Potioner and elixirs master.

Special Skills: Acting normal.

Weapons: Pain potions, acid grenades, scalpel.

Tableau: An aged, cloaked man holding a lantern in the dark.

Icon: A glowing lantern.

Unique Arcana Characteristics: Appears elderly when using his powers.

Before Flash: Escalating kidnapper and serial killer.

FORTUNE (X)

Azara "Zara" Bonifácio Félix, Our Lady of Chance

"Where she stops, nobody knows."

A.k.a.: Lady Luck, the Luck Thief, Fluke

Powers: Luck absorption. Can impart misfortune (increasing her own luck) and steal luck through touch.

Special Skills: Expert pilot, trained combat fighter, markswoman.

Weapons: Helicopters. Firearms used in aerial assaults.

Tableau: A girl standing in the center of a huge spinning wheel. A sphinx runs on top of it and a dragon clings to the bottom while ancient clay dice rain down from a night sky.

Icon: Wheel.

Unique Arcana Characteristics: Eyes and veins turn purple when she establishes a luck conduit.

Before Flash: Brazilian heiress to Dragão Novo, the largest turbine helicopter manufacturer in São Paulo State (the civilian helicopter capital of the world).

SÃO PAULO, BRAZIL
DAY 0

Kicked back at my father's desk, I daydreamed about my new flame-thrower and took in the view from his office's floor-to-ceiling glass wall. The city streets sprawled below.

He should be finished soon with the group of Japanese investors. He'd wanted me to join him in the conference room, but I had heard his sales pitch a thousand times: "In São Paulo, kidnappings among the wealthy have become a way of life. Here, we live in armored, guarded penthouses and travel by helicopter from one tower to the next. If the same happens in your city, will you be ready?"

Yes, there were kidnappings here; my own mother had been murdered during an abduction. Yes, our copters sold like crazy. But he might be overplaying the facts a touch.

Most traveled via copter to escape the miserable traffic.

His fearmongering worked for me. Nobody benefited from Dragão's sales like I did. Money enabled me to buy things like flamethrowers.

God, I loved fire.

"Where is your mind, daughter?" Papai asked, smiling at me from his office door. Behind him, his assistant ushered the investors toward the rooftop helipad. One of our pilots would fly them out.

I rose to give Papai his seat back, then hopped up on the corner of his desk. "I was thinking about my trip. I leave tonight."

He sank into his chair. "Or you could shadow me at work this week instead."

We'd had this talk repeatedly. He wanted me to concentrate on our business. At twenty-three, I was a skilled pilot, a crack shot, and a trained fighter, but I wouldn't know a spreadsheet if it came at me with a machete. "I have a solid lead on the Oliveras." Once I located their hideout, I would torch it with my new toy.

When I was eleven, they'd killed my mother. I'd been hunting them for the last year, ever since I'd come into my Dragão stock shares. With money, I'd funded more training, weapons, and a crew.

My life had been shaped by revenge, and I possessed the ideal temperament for it. Papai had once said I'd been born bloodthirsty; he wasn't wrong.

Now he exhaled, looking older than his years. He was athletic and fit, but stress beat him down. "How can you keep chasing this vendetta?"

My notorious temper redlined like a straining turbine engine. "How can you *not?*" Rumor held that Papai had gotten his start as a criminal, running his own crew before he'd married Mamãe. If I were him, I'd be drawing on my roots to avenge her. "They murdered your wife. By your reaction, I have to wonder if you loved her at all."

Fury flashed in his eyes. "I *worshipped* her."

Everyone had. After her passing, my grandmother had died of grief, my grandfather drinking himself into an early grave. The last thing he'd told me: "If you want justice for your mother, you'll have to deliver it yourself." I'd been fourteen.

I would make the Olivera clan pay for all three deaths.

Papai said, "If you continue to go after them, sooner or later they will strike back against my only child and heir. Then I would retaliate, and this war would last forever, until we're all destroyed."

"I *wish* they would come after me." Even now I had a Glock in a holster on my back and a tactical blade tucked in my boot.

My handpicked crew and I had already taken out two Olivera sons. Now I hunted for the rest of that generation, but especially for Bento Olivera, their father.

He was the one who'd slit my mother's throat—*after* Papai had paid the ransom.

My hand drifted to my pistol. Merely touching the weapon cooled some of my fury, focusing it. "I'm not getting into this with you again. I just stopped by to tell you I'm leaving."

The fire alarm blared to life.

I stood, wary. We were fifty floors up. I only liked fire when it didn't threaten *me*. "What's happening?"

"I don't know." Papai pulled up security feeds on his computer screen. Employees were filing out downstairs. The investors had boarded on the helipad, were about to dust off.

Papai assessed the feeds. "No sign of fire. Perhaps we should get to the safe room."

"Which one?" We had two—one at ground level for fires or natural disasters and one on this floor for an enemy incursion or attack.

"My instinct tells me to get low." Papai had a sense for such things. He glanced toward his bookcase. Behind it was the entrance to this floor's safe room and the private elevator. "We should chance the elevator."

I nodded. "Let's go—" *Bam!* Something had crashed into the glass wall.

A bird? It'd left a smear of blood and feathers. Then another one hit the glass. And another. Half a dozen birds had flown straight into it. "How weird." Above the blood, I spied brightness. "Papai, look!" The most beautiful bands of light wavered in the night sky. They shimmered green and purple over the mountains.

He turned to the glass wall and sucked in a breath. "Extraordinary." Side by side, we watched the lights.

I murmured, "I could look at them forever."

The Dragão copter with the investors had taken off and now hovered just in front of us, blocking my view of the lights, irritating me. I supposed the pilot was just as entranced.

Another copter drifted toward it. Those pilots were going to tangle if they weren't careful. They coasted even closer. The Dragão pilot made no move to evade. *Closer.* "Papai?" *Closer.*

He didn't answer, completely caught up in the lights.

Closer! "Papai!"

Their rotor blades snarled. Turbines whined as the copters pitched toward this building. Toward *this* wall.

One was coming in nose first, the other tail first. "Look out!"

I shoved Papai out of the way just before the impact—

Rotor blades hit; glass shattered in a deafening crash.

Shards of it plugged the walls. One spike shot past me, missing my throat by a hairbreadth.

"Zara!" Papai had gotten to the door.

I was trapped between live blades! One copter's tail boom swung through the office, its smaller rotor like a mower. It chewed up anything in its path; paper and debris sailed in a vortex, my hair whipping my face and eyes. *Can't see!*

Something nailed my side. "Ahh!" The force knocked me off my feet—onto my front, punching the air from my lungs. A sharp stake of wood clattered to the floor beside me.

I wasn't gored? The wood had struck my gun! I flung myself over and scuttled backward till I met the wall.

All at once the air cleared—because that tail rotor was upon me! No time to make it to my feet. To run. *Trapped.*

As if in slow motion, the tail boom swept toward me.

"Zara, get down!" Papai yelled from the doorway.

I pressed myself flat on my back and turned my head a split second before the rotor blades floated above my face. Whirring metal skimmed my ear by millimeters. I screamed and screamed, my voice distorted by the rotation.

Then . . . clear. I stared in shock as the tail continued past me.

"Come, Zara! Run now!"

He held open the door with one arm, cradling his side with the other. Injured? Blood soaked the side of his button-down and streaked down his face.

I struggled to my feet, lungs heaving smoky air. The smell of aviation fuel reeked; the wasted blades still spun. I glanced at the bookcase, at our exit; blocked by the Dragão copter's fuselage.

Survivors were trapped inside. They yelled, begging us for help. They should be afraid—what was left of the blades might catch the floor and lever them out the window, like a tire jack. Or the engine could ignite all that fuel.

I lurched toward Papai, following along the wall. Shards of glass jutted from it like a porcupine's quills.

We limped away from the crash, heading toward the far side of the floor's soaring atrium.

"Are you hurt?" he asked.

"I'm fine." But he wasn't. "What happened to you?"

"Splinters from the desk." He looked me over. "How could you not have a scratch on you?"

I shook my head. "No idea."

With a last *thunk thunk!* those rotors finally caught and stalled. The men were screaming and pounding on the doors. Had the copter shifted to the edge of the room? Maybe they dangled. If not, they'd been lucky.

The building's power flickered; emergency lights blinked to life. The alarm stuttered, going to an intermittent buzz.

A scorching gust of wind rocked the building, filtering in through that missing wall to reach Papai and me. The glass ceilings and walls of the atrium groaned all around us.

Though the air was hot, I got chills across my nape. "Listen. What is that?"

"The alarm?"

"No. Louder." I heard a . . . roar?

The sky grew lighter and lighter. Neighboring high-rises swayed in the wind. Beneath my feet, this floor trembled. Papai and I shared a look. We were at the very top of the tallest structure in the city—in a glass atrium.

As the focal point, we'd proudly staged our latest-model copter in the air; it swung above us.

Papai murmured, *"Meu Deus,"* yanking my attention from the copter.

What looked like a giant laser was coming for us. A shock wave blasted the windows of other buildings as it approached. "Papai?"

"It must be a bomb. We have to reach the ground! Head for the stairs!"

As we ran past the door to his office, I glanced over. The survivors frantically kicked at the copter's door; just as we crossed, the wreckage was blown against the doorway. The fuselage crumpled like a tin can; blood splashed the windshield interior. The copter plugged the doorway hole, but the impact still rocked us, tossing Papai and me to the floor.

Behind us, the atrium shattered.

We crawled down the gallery toward the stairwell. "Keep going!" he said from ahead of me. "Do not slow! And do not look back at the light."

The building quaked. Beside me, a bronze statue of Papai toppled over. I scrambled forward. *Never make it.* I braced for the impact—but the opposite wall had buckled, *catching* the statue's head! Like a crumbly pillow. The length of bronze was suspended right above me, held aloft by that failing wall.

I scurried; the statue dropped. *Boom!*

I gazed back in shock. It'd landed centimeters from my feet. "Did you see that?" I asked Papai. The odds of dodging that must be a million to one.

"Keep going!"

We reached the stairwell door. He levered himself to his feet, then grabbed my hand to pull me up.

When our skin made contact, his eyes widened; mine narrowed. We'd both felt some kind of energy pass between us.

"What was that?" I asked.

He blinked, staring into my eyes. "I-I don't know." He helped me inside the stairwell. "We have to keep moving."

"I'm waiting on you." I took off.

We dashed down the stairs. He was in shape, keeping up with me despite his injuries. We'd made it down three flights when the building quaked again. The stairwell seemed to contract on itself, walls cracking.

A ceiling tile popped open above Papai; electrical cords and wiring dropped—just in time to snare his neck!

I cried, "Papai!" I attacked the sparking wires, unraveling them to free him.

Pale with shock and confusion, he rubbed his throat. The building continued shaking, vibrations beneath our feet. "Just . . . just keep going! We won't be safe till we're on the ground." He shoved me ahead of him. "Go!"

A few more flights down, another quake rocked us. This time the stairwell expanded with an eruption of wall fissures.

A piece of metal swung from the ceiling, arcing just past my ear. Sprinkler pipe? I turned back, saw it crash into the fire-extinguisher cabinet. The loosed extinguisher dropped directly on his foot.

The building seemed bent on destroying him!

"Porra," he yelled in pain.

"Let me help you!"

Limping forward, he snapped, "Go." He gritted his teeth, using one leg and the railing to hop down the stairs.

We descended dozens more flights without problems. Finally we reached the last one.

"We're here!" Three steps from the bottom, I stopped to wait, keeping an eye on him above.

"I'm right behind you. Head for the safe—"

The railing broke loose, tumbling over. I screamed as he plummeted past me. The railing edge brushed my jacket, missing me by a whisper.

He landed on the steps with one leg tangled in the bars, groaning in pain.

I scrambled over to him. *"Papai!"*

His face was bloody, his eyes dazed. Blood seeped from his side, oozing down the steps. "Think I broke my leg."

I strained to lift the railing. Too heavy. I attempted again, barely budging it. "You have to help me—we have to free you."

"Zara, wh-when this attack ends, take the long-range copter. Fly north. Get to my brother in Texas."

"I'm not leaving you!"

"The building will come down. Rescuers will find you. But it will be too late for me."

"Don't talk like that, Papai!"

His face was tense from pain. "I must confess to you. . . . I have robbed you."

"What are you talking about?"

"The Olivera clan. Bento Olivera found out something I'd done. . . . I-I wronged him first."

"What did you do?" What *could* Papai have done to warrant my mother's murder? I knelt beside him, impatient for his answer as he struggled to speak.

"They took your mother because . . . I kidnapped his wife years before."

Olivera retaliated? "Why did you? For money?"

He nodded, then winced with pain. The rumors of Papai's criminal background had been true. "The woman fought me . . . I didn't mean . . . the gun went off. Bullet in her spine."

The breath whooshed from my lungs. I'd thought Bento had selected Mamãe out of a thousand wealthy women in the city. I'd never been able to wrap my mind around the randomness—as if my mother had been betrayed by chance, as if her life had ended when her luck had run out.

But she'd been *targeted.* "Why would you let me hunt them? Without telling me?"

"I wanted to, so many times. But I didn't want you to hate me. The lie took on a life of its own."

This revelation stunned me as much as anything else I'd seen tonight. "I believed they'd taken her because they were greedy pigs!" And so I had gutted Bento's sons like pigs. *After* I'd tortured them.

"No. Revenge."

The Oliveras never would have stopped. Because of my father. Fury surged inside me. "*You* started this—because *you* were greedy. My mother is dead because of you! Her parents are dead because of you!"

"And I will go to hell for my sins." Almost to himself, he said, "Parted from her forever."

I still would have gone after the Oliveras, but I wouldn't have *toyed* with them. That family had only been avenging a loved one.

As I had been. Their crime was the same as mine. "I wanted to punish the one responsible for her death." My fists clenched. "Why should I not kill *you*?"

He murmured, "Think that will happen all on its own, daughter."

Another quake. This one was louder and more intense than the previous ones—and it was mounting.

"Leave me," Papai ordered. "Get to the safe room!"

The ground shook so hard, I tottered on my feet. I turned toward the exit, but the door wouldn't open. The frame was skewed, wedging the door shut.

Stone cracked; metal groaned. I swallowed, gazing up the stairwell. The stairs swayed. Because the *building* was swaying.

It shifted side to side, more and more violently, until suddenly it wobbled and . . . dropped.

Oh, *meu Deus*, the entire fucking thing was coming down!

A cloud of dust and debris exploded downward like an avalanche. I hunched, covering my head.

Full dark.

As the rubble settled, stones knocked against each other. A stray *crack!* sounded. The air was thick with dust, my lungs filled with it.

"Papai?" I coughed and pulled my shirt over my face, breathing through the fabric. "Papai, answer me."

Nothing. I fished my phone out of my pocket and clicked on the flashlight. I gaped at what I saw.

Rubble had piled up all around me—even above me—a perfect cocoon.

Except for the sole rock that had breached it.

The one that had bashed in my father's head.

Somehow I was . . . untouched.

THE FURY (XI)

Spite, She Who Harrows

"Blood will tell. Blood will run.
But the tears of the damned always taste sweet."

A.k.a.: Justice

Powers: Acid spitting and flight. Superhuman senses, strength, and healing. Infrared vision. Her fireproof wings can blend into surroundings, camouflaging her.

Special Skills: Concealment.

Weapons: Razor-sharp claws that tip her wings and a scourging whip.

Tableau: A blind-folded winged demoness, holding a steel-studded whip in her upraised right hand and weighing scales in her lowered left hand.

Icon: Navy-blue scales.

Unique Arcana Characteristics: Her eyes are yellow instead of white, with green keyhole pupils. She has long retractable claws and batlike wings. Prior to striking an enemy, her wings will vibrate, the sharp claws tapping each other to make a rattling sound.

Before Flash: Daughter of Egyptian museum curators, in the States for a long-term exhibit.

SUBURB OF CHICAGO, ILLINOIS
DAY 0

Look at the lights! The newscasters had talked about these right before the channels all cut out.

Lines of purples and pinks and greens rolled like waves in the night sky. So beautiful I could cry.

I heard others on my street oohing and aahing. Most were American hipsters; all of them behaved as if I didn't exist. Nothing new.

My parents did as well.

But tonight I didn't ridicule my neighbors as usual—because I actually had something in common with them.

We were all basking in these lights.

No one had told me I might see the aurora borealis this time of year. I could stare at it forever. I adjusted my thick glasses and wondered if my parents were watching from their ritzy uptown patron party.

As usual, I was babysitting my little sister, Febe. I thought of her solemn brown eyes, plump cheeks, and eight-year-old lisp, and considered heading back to our rented house to get her. She was in the basement playing video games, would never see the sky on her own.

She was the only one in the world I loved, the only one who didn't view my usual expression as sneering or vindictive. She had never called me the nickname that somehow followed me from country to country: *Spiteful.*

I exhaled. Still staring over my shoulder, I headed toward the house. But when I had to walk under a tree, I couldn't bring myself to lose my view of the lights—

Pain flared, shooting across my upper back. What was *that?*

Ignore it! All I wanted to do was look at the sky. . . . Another jolt ripped through me. My legs gave way, my knees hitting the sidewalk.

I managed to cry, "H-help me!" to my closest neighbors, but they were captivated by the lights.

My skin felt as if it was being stabbed, but from the inside. It was . . . it was *ripping open*!

I heard wet sounds, like something being born. A wave of nausea swept through me, and I vomited black liquid all over the pavement. Cloth was tearing somewhere nearby—and then these bloody, gooey black things flapped in front of me. I shrieked, scrambling away from them.

They followed me! I'd never outrun them; I cowered down—and they stopped. Then quivered when I timidly started to rise. Because they were . . . attached to my body? Ah God, they'd sprung out of my back!

My lips parted with shock. The things unfolding around me were . . . "W-wings." They were huge and shaped like a bat's, just like the ones that had haunted my dreams ever since I could remember.

But the lights in the sky . . . must look at them!

Those wings opened wide, blocking the view above, the only thing I wanted to see. Just as I realized I was losing my mind, the wings enfolded me tightly.

Like a shroud.

I wanted out! These stupid things were keeping me from the lights! I raked my nails against the velvety surface to get free; more pain shot through me. Were my nails getting sharper? The grayish flesh on the underside of these wings was as sensitive as my fingertips.

I punched them, wrestling against them. After struggling for what must have been an eternity, I accepted that I couldn't escape.

The appeal of the lights had lessened, anyway. Now I was overwhelmed with the need to get to Febe. What if she went upstairs and realized she was all alone?

I mentally willed my new appendages to retract. . . . Nothing. I was trapped, a caterpillar in her cocoon.

And like a caterpillar, I began changing.

Molting.

Even in the enclosed darkness, I could somehow see—in fact, my glasses no longer helped my vision, actually *obscured* it. So I crushed them in my palm. Seeing with perfect clarity for the first time, I watched my nails grow into long sharp claws and my skin thicken into scales.

I wasn't as shocked by these changes as I would've expected.

My mind turned to a memory from eight years ago, when I'd been Febe's age. I'd watched a teenage boy from my neighborhood stroll hand in hand into the forest with a girl—though he'd already been in a relationship with another one.

I'd followed the couple, hiding in a tree. When they'd started having sex, I'd thought of his betrayed girlfriend and imagined the pain his unfaithfulness would bring her.

Bile had risen in my throat. I'd wanted so badly to punish him that I'd gnashed my teeth and my body had begun to shake. I'd fallen, dislocating my shoulder.

They'd called me Spiteful (as usual) and left me there.

Getting to a doctor had taken forever. The pain in my shoulder had faded after a while, replaced by a dull feeling of *wrongness.*

Now, as I witnessed my body evolving, I realized my new form was *rightness.* Something wrong had finally clicked into place.

For all of my sixteen years, my life had been dislocated. I understood that now.

Outside my cocoon, my surroundings were transforming as well. Heat seared the backs of my wings. I smelled flames and soot. I sensed fires, chaos, and destruction. Once I finally got free, would anything still be standing?

Would Febe still be alive . . . ?

Molting must have depleted me; even though I felt gripping fear for my sister, I couldn't keep my eyes open.

Sleep took me. Dreams arose. I saw myself spitting acid at foes and soaring through the sky with my new wings. I'd be able to defend myself with them; large hook-shaped claws tipped the ends of the largest flares. They would be razor sharp—

My eyes flashed open, and I was instantly awake. How long had I been asleep? Must've been hours. *Movement nearby.*

I sensed it as a predator would. Moaning sounded directly outside my cocoon. I could perceive wetness against my wings.

Moaning and . . . slime. *Enemy,* my new instinct told me. *Destroy.*

I needed to annihilate anything that came so close to me when I was vulnerable. I pictured using my wings to kill. I would corral my enemies with my large left wing, keeping them trapped as I struck with my right one.

This made perfect sense to me. *Rightness.*

At last the tight folds around me eased. My wings began to vibrate, the weighty hook claws tapping each other to make a rattling sound.

Like a snake, I was signaling that a predator prepared to strike. The sound pleased me, my own purr. I'd never killed before, but already I could tell I would enjoy it.

All was rightness in the world.

I leapt up, wings flashing out, knocking away people as I positioned myself. Wait—not *people.* Not anymore. They'd been turned into monstrous-looking creatures with filmy white eyes. Some more than others, all of them getting worse. They wore regular clothes, but their skin had the texture of a battered paper bag, as if they'd spent a thousand straight years in a tanning bed.

I readied to exterminate these bag-skinned creatures with my claws, and a sense of satisfaction hit me. This was what I was meant to do. No wonder I'd always felt like an outsider. I'd always *been* one.

I beheaded the first, then another. And another.

I recognized two things: I was as much a monster as these creatures. And I didn't enjoy killing; I adored it.

Behind them, the neighborhood was mostly gone. Only brick houses here or there still stood. The rest was ash. I sucked in a breath. Including my family's house.

Febe had been in the basement; she might have survived! *Must get to her.*

These things kept blocking me. As I downed more of them, I heard Febe's scream.

She did live! I used my wings to shove creatures aside as I rushed toward the remains of our home. I spotted her in the dark, could detect the warmth of her little body—as if I had infrared vision.

She was running from one of those bag creatures, wending between flaming trees. Her eyes were blank with terror. The red glow of her heart was racing; I could see it.

We met gazes. She was just as terrified of me. *Must explain. . . .*

Leaping upward, I clumsily flapped my wings until they scooped smoky air—like sails catching a breeze—holding me aloft.

Getting accustomed. Easier now. I was flying! Ah, the rightness!

Where was Febe? There!

I landed a few feet in front of her, holding up my palms. She skidded to a stop, horrified, clearly not recognizing me.

I parted my lips. A clear liquid streamed out of my mouth; it spattered her face.

Acid? As in my dreams. Her flesh sizzled, her eyes and features disintegrating. Her shriek pierced the night.

Wrongness.

THE HANGED MAN (XII)

[INACTIVATED CARD]*

██████████, Our Lord Uncanny

"Never ████████ *I* ████████*"*

A.k.a.: ██████████

Powers: ████████████████████████████
████████████████████████████
████████████████

Special Skills: ████████████████

Weapons: ██████████

Tableau: ████████████████████████████
████████████████

Icon: ████████████

Unique Arcana Characteristics: ████████████

Before Flash: ██████████████████████
████████████████████

DAY 0

*Details hidden by the Fool.

THE TOWER (XVI)

Joules, Lord of Lightning

"Eyes to the skies, lads, I strike from above!"

A.k.a.: Master of Electricity

Powers: Can generate and control electrical energy. Can electrify his skin and create javelins that transform into lightning bolts.

Special Skills: Precise aiming and superhuman throwing. Singing.

Weapons: Silver javelins engraved with esoteric symbols.

Tableau: Lightning striking a turret, sending people falling.

Icon: Lightning bolt.

Unique Arcana Characteristics: Sparking skin.

Before Flash: A choirboy from Ireland in New York for a singing competition.

TEMPERANCE (XIV)

Calanthe, Collectress of Sins

"Crush you with the Weight of Sins."

A.k.a.: Sin, Collectress of Evils

Powers: Sin detection and pathokinesis (emotion manipulation). Her Weight of Sins power can magnify another's guilt and horror over past deeds. Is immune to the Empress's poisons. Enhanced senses, healing, throwing, and precise aiming.

Special Skills: Guile, social adaption.

Weapons: A pair of sai, hand-held martial-arts weapons with three prongs

Tableau: Androgynous robed figure standing on a pedestal, pouring water from one chalice to another; the sun and a bolt of lightning glow in the background.

Icon: A gold chalice.

Unique Arcana Characteristics: When she utilizes her power, a haze erupts around her and ripples of energy seem to flow from her, bombarding her target.

Before Flash: High-school student from India, living in the States with her older sister, a chronicler.

NEW YORK SUBWAY PLATFORM
DAY 0

"What were you *thinking* not to sleep with that boy?"

I sat on a bench, flinching as Diya railed at me on the phone. I could picture my sister pacing in our apartment, narrowed eyes flashing with anger.

"I thought I'd convinced him to stay," I told her.

Yet with his shoulders back and face stoic, Joules had left me, boarding the train to head to the airport for his flight home.

"You gave him no reason to stay, Calanthe." Diya made a frustrated sound. "You could have locked down an alliance with the Tower!"

My card's MO was to seek out a stronger player in the beginning of the game, exchanging the knowledge from my chronicles for that card's strength.

Until I could do away with him or her.

As with most Arcana, my ability grew as the game stretched on. The majority of players didn't *want* to harm others, at least not until the heat of battle was upon them, and the guilt was debilitating; my Weight of Sins power was directly proportional to their sense of guilt.

No matter what, I needed the Tower's help to challenge Death. As long as the Reaper lived, we were all just walking corpses anyway.

"Joules told me he loved me," I said. But he'd loved his large family back in Ireland more.

"Naturally. Because he wanted to sleep with you."

Yes, but only after a certain stipulation had been met. Would Diya laugh if I told her what he'd always planned?

She exhaled. "Something will pull him back into the game. He'll converge with the rest of you." Diya knew these things; our ailing mother had trained her to be my chronicler, handing down our line's Arcana chronicles into Diya's capable hands.

But how would Joules get back to me from across the Atlantic? Especially if some catastrophe loomed?

Diya said, "I just wonder if you made enough of a lasting impression to forge an unbreakable alliance."

So did I. . . .

TWO WEEKS AGO

I was on my way home from the dojo when a bus wheezed to a stop in front of my neighborhood's Catholic cathedral. A banner rippling above the church doors read: INTERNATIONAL CHORUS COMPETITION. A group of about thirty teenage boys in magenta gowns began filing off the bus, chattering and laughing as they made their way into the church.

Choirboys? I snorted with derision.

Until my gaze lit upon one kid among them. He had reddish-brown hair and dark eyes, and he was thin. Compared to the others, he looked poor. His ill-fitting gown had been mended repeatedly, his red collar was faded, and he was in need of a haircut. His shoes were polished but worn out, and his high-riding pant cuffs clearly were *not* meant to be a style statement.

So why did I find this unremarkable kid compelling—

An image flickered over him: lightning striking a stone castle tower and people falling from the turret. I was seeing . . . a tableau. My eyes went wide. He was an Arcana!

And not just any random card. He was *the Tower.*

One of the mightiest of all the Major Arcana was a scrawny choirboy!

I shouldn't be surprised by this encounter. As Diya had told me again and again, there was no such thing as "random" in the game. We were all thrown together.

Wait till she heard that I'd already found the Tower! This news would certainly cheer her up. Pensive about whatever catastrophe would soon befall us, she hated being separated from our older mother, and she despised New York.

The Tower caught sight of me and did a double take. Maybe he was seeing a faint hint of my own tableau. Maybe he was the same as all the other guys checking out my outfit: tight boy-short pants, a sports bra, and an open hoodie. The Empress wasn't the only one with mesmerizing looks.

And I had more guile than all the others combined.

He looked to be about sixteen, my age. I wondered if he knew anything about the Arcana. Players usually didn't. I could lock this choirboy down in an alliance before the game even began! He'd be putty.

I leaned against a light post. Twirling the end of my ponytail, I cast him a flirtatious smile.

He glanced over one shoulder, then the other. Frowning, he hiked a thumb at his chest.

I pointed at him and mouthed: *Yes, you.*

His lips parted.

I crooked my finger at him, and he started for me immediately— until a burly priest grabbed his arm to usher the boy inside. The Tower craned his head back to keep me in sight.

As if I'd let you get away, kid.

Once I heard singing, I entered the church. Despite my skimpy outfit, I sauntered down the aisle to a front pew. Every gaze in that choir fixed on me, including the Tower's.

I took a seat and shucked off my backpack. The boys around him noticed my attention and elbowed him.

Up on a stage, with that stained-glass backdrop, he looked so . . . virtuous.

Once he and I took out Death, I would use my particular ability on the Tower. After a good boy like him turned killer, he'd have no defense against my Weight of Sins.

I pulled a notebook from my pack and scribbled some words, as dark and bold as I could. Catching his gaze, I held up the notebook and turned the pages.

You
Me
Coffee shop across street
4 today

Face gone redder than his choirboy collar had ever been, he nodded.

At twenty-five till four, he entered the shop.

I'd gotten here at three.

His eyes darted until he spotted me, sitting in the back. His cheeks grew red again, and he whirled around, suddenly enthralled with the display of coffee mugs.

He was wearing a threadbare button-down and jeans. I'd bet he'd agonized over his clothes for the first time in his life.

I waited, but he was too shy to approach me. I wondered if he'd ever even kissed a girl. I called, "Hey, choirboy."

He turned slowly, then headed toward my table. When he stood before me, he swallowed thickly.

I kicked a chair out for him. "What's your name?"

He sat. "I'm P-Patrick Joules," he said with a thick accent.

"I'm Calanthe. Where are you from?"

"Oirland."

"How old are you?"

"Fifteen," he answered. With his gaze dipping to my plunging V-neck shirt, he added, "You must be eighteen or nineteen."

I teasingly asked, "Are my boobs staring at your eyes again?"

His head snapped up, his expression mortified. If blushing could kill . . .

I grinned. "All parts of me think you have really nice eyes." He actually did. "And I'm sixteen, for the record."

He canted his head, his blush relenting a bit. He cleared his throat and said, "Wh-whereabouts are you from?"

"I was born in India, but I grew up all over the place. I've been going to high school here for two years."

When I'd turned thirteen, my sister had made me apply to exchange programs in a dozen different countries, but they'd all been full.

Miraculously, a spot had opened up here. Which had led us to believe the game would be played out in this country. Bingo. Already players were converging. "What are you in town for, *Tower*?"

He frowned. "What's that mean?"

"You don't know about the game?" I studied his face.

"Game?" His confusion deepened. When I raised my eyebrows, he said, "I don't know about any game."

When I focused on a person, I could sense his or her sins; this boy wasn't lying. "I'm just messing with you. Seriously, what are you in the States for?"

"I'm here for two weeks for a choir competition."

I leaned forward and murmured, "I think you have a sexy voice."

It broke when he asked, "C-can I buy you a cup of coffee?"

As I stared into his earnest eyes, I felt a flare of something like pity that I'd have to murder him.

But I was the Temperance Card. The Weight of Sins had never bothered me. "Only if you promise to ask me out before I finish it."

SEVEN DAYS AGO

"What do you think, choirboy?" I asked Joules, standing in the eighty-sixth-floor observatory of the Empire State Building. Lights twinkled below and beyond. A storm was rolling in—just as forecasted; all according to plan. Except for a few mugging couples, we had the place to ourselves. "Pretty cool, huh?"

He and I had seen each other as much as possible for the last week—before and after his choir practice, and every night as well when he sneaked out of his dorm. I'd taken him to my favorite haunts, trying unsuccessfully to sleep with him. He hadn't even attempted to kiss me!

"Ach, how much did it cost you for this?" he demanded. I could tell he was amped (maybe literally?) to see the city from this height, but he hadn't stopped scowling since I'd handed over our tickets.

I huffed. "Does it matter?" He always insisted on picking up the bill, though he couldn't afford it. By the way his stomach growled each afternoon, I suspected he was using his lunch money to pay for us.

Which kind of struck me as . . . romantic.

"It matters to me, Cally." That was his nickname for me; apparently it was a law in Ireland that everyone had a pet name.

"This isn't the eighteen hundreds. Girls take guys out sometimes." Even if there were no game, I'd probably want to see him. I'd been surprised by how much I'd enjoyed spending time with him.

I had so much more in common with him than with my fellow international students. They had college application essays to fill out; I had sai training. They wanted a diploma; I wanted icons.

"Those tickets must've cost you plenty for a view this grand."

"Fine. You really want to know how I paid for them?" At his nod, I told him the truth: "I marched into the guys' locker room at the dojo, snapped a photo of this one bully's junk, and blackmailed him." The guy had been so furious, I'd provoked him to charge me. At the last second, I'd stepped aside; he'd rammed a locker headfirst. Then I'd plucked a hundred from his wallet. "Let's put it this way: you and I are having pizza after."

I could all but hear Joules's thoughts: *I canna tell if she's kidding. Please, Jaysus, let her be kidding.*

I shrugged. "See? That's why you have to stay in New York. To keep me out of trouble."

More and more often, I'd broached the subject of his staying. At home, Diya was putting all kinds of pressure on me to solidify this alliance: "Bring him back to the apartment. I'll stay out all night. Get this boy locked down, Calanthe!"

Now he sighed. "I wish I could. But me mam has enough trouble with me hellion brothers." Five of them. "I should not add to her worries. Plus, I'm skint." At my frown, he explained, "Out of money. And I canna work in this country."

"You could borrow from me." Not that my sister and I had much to spare.

He scowled again. "Never'll happen."

Seeing he wouldn't be moved—for now—I said, "Then we need to enjoy every minute together." I'd been an hour early tonight, but he'd already been waiting for me.

His face had lit up when he spotted me, and he'd trotted toward me like a whipped puppy. Then, seeming to realize how silly he looked, he'd slowed and played it cool.

I tilted my head at him. "I'm the first girl you've gone out with, aren't I?"

His cheeks heated. He was cute when he blushed like that. I found myself teasing him a lot, just to get a blush out of him.

Instead of blustering (which he also did a lot), he grew solemn. "Because I had not met a lass as fine as you are."

After a few moments, I blinked, surprised that I'd been staring into his eyes. "Um, let me show you my favorite spot." I steered him to gaze out at the approaching storm. "Up here, there's all this static electricity. Can you feel it?"

His expression was excited. "I can. Is it supposed to give you a high like this?" Thunder rumbled, and a laugh escaped him.

"Hmm. Maybe some of us more than others."

A bolt of lightning flared in the distance, and he was riveted. "I've always fancied lightning."

"Have you? You're like the electrical guy from my sister's Tarot legends." I'd told him that Diya used to entertain me with tales of the Major Arcana. Easing him into my world—*our* world—I'd explained the basics of the game and most of the twenty-two players.

"The one called the Tower?" He grinned. "I thought I'd be Death for certain. Where's me scythe?"

I shivered at the mere mention of Death.

Joules gazed out as more lightning struck. "Cally, I've never felt more alive than I do right now."

"Then take a pic with me." I pulled out my phone. When he moved in closer, I put my arm around him and hammed it up for the shot.

He murmured at my ear, "Will you blackmail me with pictures too?"

I faced him. "Of course. You're going to have to stay with me."

He couldn't seem to take his eyes off my lips, so I licked them. But he didn't move in for a kiss. He'd definitely never had one before.

I said, "So young."

His eyes went wide. "No younger than you are!"

"Prove it. Kiss me."

He gazed around. "Here? Tere'll be cameras," he said, accent thickening.

"Nobody else cares."

Joules looked like he'd rather eat nails than kiss me here. But he let me maneuver him until I stood between him and the camera.

"Don't you *want* to kiss me?"

"O' course I want to, but it might lead to other tings, and I'm waiting till I'm wed." He was serious! "Cally, wait with me—"

My hand dipped down, and the almighty Tower gave a whimper. I rested my palm on the front of his jeans.

His voice broke higher as he said, *"Jaysus."*

When I moved my hand, his eyes rolled back in his head. A bolt struck nearby—as if from his emotions—and he groaned.

"Nobody waits anymore," I murmured.

"I'd always p-planned to." Another groan.

"I think you're just throwing out excuses. Maybe you don't want me to be your girlfriend."

"To have you as me lass?" He tried to steady his gaze, to meet mine, as if he was about to give me a promise. "Tere's nothing I want more! From the first second I saw you, I knew you were the one!" Though his body was shaking with need, he tugged my hand away—so he could hold it with both of his own. Gods, he was so sincere, so *virtuous.* "You're to be mine?"

A traitorous thought arose: *What if I am his?*

No, the game made that impossible. I hesitated, then lied: "I am."

His face lit with adoration, and bolts struck all around us. They reflected in his eyes.

NOW

From my subway bench, I gazed at nothing. He'd actually left me. Was I more upset that I'd lost my choirboy than I was about losing the Tower?

Ridiculous. The number-one rule of the game? Never, never develop feelings for another player. What kind of future could two cards have if they loved each other? They aged as long as the game wore on. So two possibilities existed—if they managed to eliminate all the other cards—and both were awful.

Either one would die young, or one would live old until the next game began.

Unless . . . they could rope in another Arcana to outlive them both.

I dreaded going home and facing my sister. She'd be able to see I was pining for Joules. How had he gotten under my skin in such a short time?

Maybe I'd sleep on this bench.

When a hot wind blew down the subway tunnel, I glanced up. A train was stopping. Not a single soul hopped on? Weird. I hadn't seen anyone descend the steps since Joules had boarded his train.

I'd tried everything to stop him. I'd told him, "My sister said you could stay with us. You and I can share my room."

He'd sputtered, "It would no' be right!"

I'd told him that I was dying to sleep with him, but he'd cited marriage again, adding, "What if the condom broke? How could I support a family?" Plus he hadn't wanted to disrespect my sister by doing anything under her roof.

My virtuous Catholic Irishman. I'd tried to guilt him into it, saying, "Everything has to be your way. You refuse to budge an inch. I worry about what kind of relationship we'll have." He'd looked stricken.

But he hadn't come back with me to the apartment.

Then last night, out of desperation, I'd admitted that those Tarot legends were real. I'd explained everything: his role, my role, the history, the danger. I'd told him something bad would happen soon, and he might not be able to get back to me.

He'd stabbed his fingers through his hair. "The thought of being separated from you makes me barmy!" His heart had thundered; I'd heard it, which meant my senses were sharpening, and the game was about to kick off.

"But you don't believe me," I'd said softly.

He'd exhaled. "I don't know . . . it's a lot to take in. I believe *you* believe it."

All the pleasures I'd offered him, all the manipulative tricks I'd used, and I'd failed—

"Cally?"

My head whipped around. Joules was exiting the train! My heart leapt, and I ran to him.

He clasped me in his arms, burying his face against my neck. "I've missed you this half hour, lass."

I'd missed him too! "You'll never make your flight now."

He drew back to gaze at me. "I'm not goin'." He grazed his knuckles over my cheek.

"But you're out of money."

He grinned. "Then I'll bloody well rob banks." He sounded so confident. And it was *sexy*.

"Bloody? You just cursed, choirboy."

He nodded. "I'm goin' to loosen meself up a wee bit. You were right; I was pushing for things from you and not budging an inch. That weren't fair to you."

"But what about your mother?"

"I'll tell her I found a work-study program over here. Not a lie, since I'll be working on robbery and you'll be teachin' me Boyfriend 101." In a gruff tone, he said, "I'm new to all this. Have patience with me?"

"Same here, okay?" I couldn't remember the last time I'd been this happy. I laced my hands behind his neck. "I can't believe you're staying."

"If this game is real, I need to be here to defend you. If it's not, I need to be here to help you."

My lips parted. None of my tricks had worked; but his need to protect me had brought him back.

"I'm your fella, Cally."

Something twisted in my chest. *I just . . . I just broke the number-one rule of the game.*

"And you're my lass."

"I am," I told him, and this time it was the truth. *We'll figure out the rest.* I was like one of those people in his tableau, falling headlong from the lightning-struck tower. But unlike them, I might not give a damn where or how I landed—as long as he was beside me.

He pulled me closer and leaned in. "C'mere." He pressed his lips to mine. When I felt the first tiny sparks of his electricity, I smiled into our kiss.

Until something bit my ankle.

I jerked back. "Ahhh!" A rat was scampering away.

It wasn't alone. They were bubbling up from the depths all around us.

"We're leavin'." Joules grabbed my hand and started for the exit.

A wave of rats crested over the top of the stairwell, squeaking madly and tumbling over each other in their haste. "No good! We're trapped down here!"

He pulled me to the bench, and we climbed atop it. "We'll be all right," he said, not panicked at all. He'd been much more nervous about kissing! "This'll get sorted," he told me with a confident nod.

Patrick Joules kept his cool.

Even when a spine-tingling roar up on the surface grew louder.

Even when wide-eyed dogs with trailing leashes dove down those steps, and bloodied zoo animals followed them.

Even when a silver baton appeared in his hand. . . .

THE DEVIL (XV)

Ogen, Foul Desecrator

"I'll make a feast of your bones!"

A.k.a.: El Diablo, the Bloody Foul One

Powers: Superhuman strength, animal aggression. Can morph his body, first into a colossal ogre, then into a giant. His thickened hide repels acid and poison.

Special Skills: Forging metal.

Weapons: None.

Tableau: A goat-man ogre leading tethered slaves.

Icon: Two black horns.

Unique Arcana Characteristics: Ten feet tall, a horned and hunchbacked beast with cloven feet.

Before Flash: Ohio teenager undergoing treatment for cutaneous horns and bony growths on his head.

THE STAR (XVII)

Stellan Tycho, Arcane Navigator

"I descend upon you like nightfall."

A.k.a.: The North Star, Supernova

Powers: Stellar embodiment and manipulation. Enhanced senses and night sight. Can generate stellar bombs, detonating himself to paralyze or destroy enemies. Echolocation, beacon emission, astronavigation.

Special Skills: Astronomy savant.

Weapons: None.

Tableau: A naked androgynous figure, gathering water under a bright eight-pointed star.

Icon: A white star.

Unique Arcana Characteristics: When he uses his power, his body vibrates until it grows indistinct.

Before Flash: Danish college student, traveling to Colorado to study astronomy.

KØBENHAVNS LUfTHAVN
(COPENHAGEN INTERNATIONAL AIRPORT)
DAY 0

"You have your books?" Mother asked me.

I nodded, depressed. I just wanted to get this farewell over with.

"Do you have your money for the trip over?" Father asked me.

I patted my jeans pocket. Another nod.

To everyone else, we looked like a regular family—two parents sending their oldest child to college, while five impatient younger siblings dreamed of their turn.

College was just a coincidence. In reality, I was going to the States— leaving behind my part-time job, my friends, and my potential girlfriend (two amazing dates)—to compete in a lethal game. Possibly.

More likely, this Arcana stuff was just my parents' insane fixation. Their craziness was our family's dirty little secret. Every family had one, right? Like my one friend's father who cheated on his taxes, and another one's mother who abused prescriptions.

At best, my parents were mentally ill and had no love for me.

At worst, they were sane and were forcing me into a contest that would most likely get me killed. And had no love for me. . . .

Astrid, the youngest of my siblings, whined, "Why does Stellan get to go to Colorado?"

Because my father "sensed" the game would be in the States this time. Could be worse. He could have "sensed" it'd be in Siberia.

I tweaked Astrid's chin. "Because I'm better than you," I said, joking, but my parents nodded.

Father told them, "Your brother's going to be famous for eternity."

Mother reached up to straighten my glasses, embarrassing me. "I'm so proud of you. All your study and hard work is about to pay off. From this moment on, your life will never be the same." She squeezed my shoulders as she hugged me. "Remember, take Death out first." She released me, motioning for my father and me to embrace.

He and I reluctantly complied. At my ear, he grated, "Come home with twenty-one icons, or don't come home."

Røvhul! Asshole! But I bit my tongue.

My dad considered himself a Tarosovo, a wise man of the Tarot, and my mom was supposed to be a chronicler, but neither of them was able to travel with me to record my theoretical deeds, because my parents spawned like asteroids, leaving them with a lot of kids and little money.

Then my mother had come up with a solution: "You can chronicle yourself! Use your phone to text us updates on everything you do. I'll download and organize your messages, entering them into the book."

That creepy, ancient tome: *The Chronicles of the Arcane Navigator.*

The pages were filled with accounts of betrayals and murders from centuries ago. I knew the book backward and forward, had been read the stories since I was old enough to remember. Now my "game" would be chronicled as well.

Via *text.*

"So here I go," I said, wondering if they might yet see reason. "If you stop getting updates, you'll know the Moon shot me through the heart or the Devil ate me." Or else I'd gotten sick of enabling their illness and refused to text any longer.

Mother pursed her lips. "That isn't funny, Stellan. Besides, you know better than to go up against the Moon." She chided me: "Only challenge players who must get close to you, especially in the beginning."

I gazed from her to my father. "You're really going to do this? Send me off by myself?" In their minds, the odds were against me living.

Which meant they were sending me off on a burning Viking funeral ship, except I was still alive and kicking, screaming for help.

"You think I should quit my job?" Father was reaching the limit of his patience with me, his face reddening with anger. "Maybe your mother should stop raising your siblings."

"No, I would never expect anyone *else's* life to drastically change." I'd reached the limits of my patience with him as well. We'd been arguing about this for weeks. Enough was enough.

I leaned down to kiss and hug my brothers and sisters, then told the five, "Watch each other's backs." Without another word, I headed toward the security line, ticket ready.

I made the mistake of looking back. They all smiled and waved like everything was normal. Like *they* were normal. It made *me* feel even crazier.

By the time I cleared security and hurried down the concourse, my flight was boarding. Sidling down the aisle, I found my seat and stowed my backpack. Then I took out my phone. *Updates, Mother? Be careful what you ask for.*

Stellan: First plane ride ever! Waiting for takeoff. Trying to decide which parent I hate more.

I didn't receive a response.

Stellan: Takeoff was smooth. The Viking funeral ship has sailed.

As the plane ascended, I gazed out the window and watched the fading shadow of the only home I'd ever known. Once the excitement of air travel dwindled, I nodded off. . . .

I slept the entire way to Atlanta, my connection city, waking as we were about to land. Despite the passage of hours, I was still furious with my parents. So I kept updating.

Stellan: Slept the whole flight. Drooled on passenger next seat over. Dreamed my parents were demented and had sent me to America to get murdered.

Mother: This isn't funny. Stop immediately.

I didn't stop.

Stellan: Thought about changing my next ticket from Colorado to Hollywood. Perhaps parents meant a different kind of star.

In the airport, I hurried down the escalator to catch the train between terminals, but just missed it. "Careful," an automated voice said. "Doors are closing and will not reopen. Please wait for the next train."

I took this opportunity to text my parents yet again.

Stellan: Heading toward a new terminal. Terminal can be an adjective as well as a noun. As in, *Stellan is terminal.*

No response.

When the next train arrived, I entered with everyone else and reached for an overhead strap. "Welcome aboard the plane train," another automated voice told me. "The next stop is for E gates. E as in Echo."

Echo. One of my powers was supposed to be echolocation. If I developed supernatural abilities, I would theoretically know how to use them, but so far there hadn't even been a glimmer.

Not surprising. I was eighteen and still didn't need to shave.

The train got under way, moving at a surprisingly fast—and rough—clip through an underground tunnel. Father was a mechanic who'd worked on trains for as long as I could remember. And he'd traveled as little as I had. I wondered what he would think about this automated people mover.

The lights flickered, and the car slowed. I glanced up, searching others' expressions. Was this normal?

The train rolled to a hissing stop—between terminals.

Everyone was dialing their phones like crazy. Okay, so *not* normal, then. I tried to call my parents. Circuits were busy.

The lights flickered again. On and off.

On and *off.*

Darkness.

For some reason, this unplanned stop hadn't tripped the train's emergency mode. As far as the train knew, we were still chugging along.

Cell phones lit up the interior. People cast each other nervous glances.

When the tunnel rumbled, a woman cried out.

Weren't there killer tornadoes in Georgia all the time? Great, my parents had sent me to be mangled by a twister.

One big, sweating American yanked at his T-shirt collar. The shirt read: *Orgasm Donor.* He grunted the syllables: "Clau-stro-pho-bic." With a yell, he attempted to force open the doors.

I wanted to say, "Those won't open as long as our gear is engaged."

His eyes darted. "Can't do this!"

A uniformed airport worker said, "Sir, just stay calm. They'll have this figured out soon."

"Back the fuck away from me." People cowered from him.

The air was growing stifling, as if the temperature were spiking a degree a second. Sweat dripped from Big Guy's face, soaking his shirt.

The rumbling in the tunnel increased to a substantial quake. In the distance, I thought I heard . . . a roar.

Big Guy went nuts, banging on the doors, kicking the safety glass, which cracked into a starburst but didn't give.

Light shone from farther along the tunnel. The quality and intensity of the light seemed to come from a natural source of some kind. I thought it was . . . fire. Or even sun?

Which couldn't be right. I checked the clock on my phone. Night. The sky should be getting darker.

A shrill shriek sounded. Then came an explosion. Before it could subside, there was another. And another . . . The roar was deafening.

Everyone hunched down. One man cried, "We're under attack! Those must be bombs!"

Hardly. If bombs had been dropped, we'd all be dead. And who would blanket an airport in weak bombs? I thought it was an even worse scenario: airplanes were dropping out of the sky. "They're planes," I murmured.

Even over all the commotion, some guy in a suit heard me. "And how would you know about the planes? What are you doing with that phone?"

I swallowed. "Checking the time." I stowed the phone in my pocket.

"Boy, you got yourself a weird accent," Big Guy said—in a weird accent. "Why would you say planes are dropping?"

How to explain to a man wearing an orgasm-donor T-shirt that bombs didn't make sense?

A screech drew our attention toward the front of the train, where the light was. Another train car was coasting toward us, seeming to roll with no brakes or power, just kinetic energy. A wayward train.

A ghost train.

People aimed their flashlight apps at the car. The exterior was charred black, and all the windows had been shattered. Was that *blood* splattered over the remaining shards of glass?

As the car grated past us, it dragged a chunk of a plane's fuselage.

Evidence that planes had dropped.

All eyes turned to me—as if *I* had done that. I raised my hands. Big Guy looked like he was about to murder me with his meaty fists.

"I'm just a student. I-I didn't have anything to do with this!"

Big Guy had followers now. As he and two other men stalked closer, I felt some odd force building inside me.

"Don't come any closer!" My hands shook, my body vibrating with energy. *Something* was happening.

Was I truly the Star?

My mind flashed to my chronicles. *Nova. Supernova. Super-luminous supernova. Stellar-mass black hole. Inburst. Outburst. Nuclear fusion.*

Cataclysm.

"I-I don't want to have an outburst! Please, stay back." They didn't. That energy inside me seemed to draw in on itself. Soon it would demand an outlet. "Please! I don't want to hurt you!"

Big Guy's eyes went wild. "So you *did* have something to do with this!"

"Nooo!" I felt like I was about to explode! My raised hands vibrated so fast, I couldn't make them out. Just two blurs. My jaw dropped at the sight.

Big Guy seized the front of my shirt. *Mistake.*

Luminescent matter erupted from me like a shock wave. *"Ahhh!"*

In horror, I watched a blue light vaporize everyone before I lost consciousness. . . .

Slow to wake. What a bizarre dream.

Something hard was gouging my side. Had I fallen asleep with a book in my bed? I frowned. Was that . . . metal? I opened my eyes.

Ah, God, I lay on tracks! Naked? I shot upright. Dread coursed through me as I craned my head around.

The train! My breath strangled in my throat. What was *left* of the train.

The exterior had exploded, metal furling outward, like a tin can blown up by dynamite.

I gaped at the wreckage, imagining my next text to my parents: You were right about everything.

THE MOON (XVIII)

Selena Lua, Bringer of Doubt

"Behold the Bringer of Doubt."

A.k.a.: The Huntress, La Luna

Powers: Pathokinesis (emotion manipulation). Can cause doubt and use moonlight as a lure. Enhanced speed, endurance, senses, dexterity, healing. Precise aiming and superhuman archery.

Special Skills: Motorcycling, marksmanship.

Weapons: Long bow, sword, firearms, whatever's handy.

Tableau: A glowing goddess of the hunt with red-tinged skin, poised in moonlight.

Icon: Quarter moon superimposed over a full moon.

Unique Arcana Characteristics: Skin glows red like a hunter's moon.

Before Flash: Motocross champion, Olympic archery hopeful, and college student who just moved away from her aunts' home.

HIGHLAND UNIVERSITY CAMPUS
DAY 0

2:01 A.M.

As I lay paralyzed in a lacrosse player's bed that smelled of sweat and stale beer, I listened to four players debate who would get "first dibs."

On *me*.

I willed my muscles to work. None did.

I mentally screamed for my eyes to open. They refused.

All I could do was lie there, helpless, and replay the events that had gotten me to this point.

THREE WEEKS AGO

"Of course you're not leaving, Lena." Aunt Wanda adjusted her glasses, her nervous tell. "You belong here with us."

"Why would *you* go to college?" Aunt Sharon demanded. She was as confident as Wanda was nervous. "The only things you need to learn concern the game."

Always with the game! I might've been cursed to be the Moon Card, the Bringer of Doubt—but that didn't mean a normal life was *im*possible.

My card was associated with longing. No more. I was sick and tired of not having friends to talk to, not having a boyfriend, not doing any of the normal stuff teenagers got to do. Resolved, I shook my head. "I'm going." I pushed past them out the front door.

They followed, stopping short at the sight of my new black Tahoe.

Sharon snapped, "Where did you get that? You don't have access to your trust fund for years."

Shoulders back, I said, "I traded in Dad's bikes." God, I'd agonized over that decision. He'd won some of his most famous motocross races on them. But I figured he and Mom would've wanted me to use them to get out from under Sharon and Wanda's rule.

I tossed my bow case inside the SUV, then headed back toward the house. I only had a one more trip.

Sharon followed alongside me, the breeze ruffling her long dark hair. "We forbid you to leave." Wanda trailed, wringing her hands.

I laughed. "I'm eighteen." And stronger than a dozen women put together. "You can't forbid shit." I stopped at the front door and asked them, "Why would you begrudge me this when we all know I'm probably gonna die soon?"

Die meant *lose.* That kind of thinking was blasphemy to them.

Sharon's expression turned fierce. "No, you will *win!*"

And if I did, what would immortality do for me? Just bring me more longing. Endless helpings of it.

In a firmer tone, I said, "The game will begin soon." I'd already started hearing the calls, and some of my powers were blooming (otherwise I never would've believed these two about the game). "If some disaster is about to strike, I plan to experience real life before then."

Though we lived in a mansion and they'd taken me all over the world, I didn't have a single friend to text. I'd never been on an official date.

"Yes, a disaster *is* coming!" Wanda cried. "That's why you need to stay close to us. We've prepared for every possible scenario." The two were secret preppers.

"You're not listening to me! Just forget it." I went inside and jogged up the steps to my room. Snagging my suitcase, I took one last look around, then returned to the landing.

They hovered at the foot of the stairs. As I bounded down, Sharon said, "Just think about what you're doing."

I'd thought of little else, from the day I'd turned eighteen.

For the past nine years, I'd obeyed their orders blindly—mental and physical training for ten hours a day, following a strict diet, never socializing—but in the last year, I'd started to wonder about them.

When I was nine, I'd heard them arguing with my mom. They'd wanted more access to me, but my parents had limited my visits to their home to one night every few weeks. On one of those nights, my family's home had burned down.

With my parents in it.

When I shimmied past them, Wanda said, "Very well. If you must go to college, we'll move there with you. We can get a house prepared—"

"Half of the reason I'm leaving is to get away from you!" I kept walking.

"People out there aren't like us." Sharon dogged my heels. "They won't care about you. We're the only ones who will always have your back."

I faced them. "Like you had my parents'?" There. I'd said it.

I'd adored my folks. I'd adored my childhood with them. If my aunts had stolen them from me . . .

Wanda and Sharon were Arcana fanatics—one a chronicler, one a Tarasova. They worshipped the game, worshipped my place in it. My parents had stood in the way of my training.

Sharon smoothly asked, "What on earth are you talking about, Lena?"

With my enhanced hearing coming online, I detected the slightest change in her breath and tone. Was this because my accusation had shocked her? Or because she was lying? I turned to Wanda. "Did the two of you burn down our home?"

"Of course not!" Her eyes went wide. "Do you really think we could murder our sister?"

The idea sounded so ridiculous when she said it like that. So why couldn't I shake my suspicion?

"This is all moot," Sharon said. "You can't afford tuition without your trust fund. Your father's bikes will only take you so far."

"Then it's a good thing I got an archery scholarship." Their faces paled at that. "Really, *duh*. As soon as I expressed interest, the school took care of everything."

Wanda's gaze darted as she cast about for something to say. "You think it's easy to make friends and fit in? You're a goddess among mortals; they will want to hurt you. It's easier not to put yourself in their sights."

I rolled my eyes. "So I should never make a friend—just because you two decided not to put yourselves out there? Just because you'll never have relationships or lives of your own?"

In a tone ringing with finality, Aunt Sharon said, "If you go, you will fail."

"Will I? Don't you two get it? You will never make the Moon Card *doubt herself*."

SIX DAYS AGO

"You're Selena, right?" some chick asked me after history class.

I drew up short. "That's me."

She smiled widely. "I'm Candy Sanderson. Really great to meet you." We shook hands.

It's happening! I'd only been in school for two weeks, already dominating discussions and turning in extra credit, and now I might be about to make a friend. *Be cool, Lena!*

"I was wondering why you didn't rush this summer."

As in sorority rush? "Never really thought about it."

"I'm not trying to be stalker-y, but I heard you're a varsity athlete, and you're obviously committed to your classes. We're always looking for cute girls with good grades and athletics. But especially the good grades, so our chapter doesn't get put on probation!" She laughed. "You should consider the spring rush."

"Yeah. I'll give it some thought." I figured I wasn't exactly sorority material, and it might interfere with my archery "practice" (which consisted of me showing up and acting like I couldn't hit the bull's-eye every time). But if one friend was good, an entire pledge class would be even better.

Candy said, "There's a rager Saturday at the lacrosse team's house. You want to go with me?"

Be cool, be cool! "Yeah, that sounds fun."

THREE HOURS AGO

"Chug, chug!" everybody around the table chanted.

All eyes were on me as I downed my Solo cup. My partner, Brian, the captain of the lacrosse team, and I were crushing it in beer pong. Was there ever an easier target? I'd forced myself to miss a shot, losing control of the table, but I'd get it back now.

After gulping the last swig, I grinned at Candy on the sidelines. She smiled back with a little less enthusiasm than earlier.

When we'd first gotten to the party, she'd introduced me to everyone like I was her new best friend, telling them I'd be rushing.

The Moon had been over the moon.

Candy had grown less possessive when I'd started cutting up with the lacrosse players like I was each one's long-lost girlfriend.

I got the sense that she'd wanted me to shine—just not this much.

But I was the Moon. Shining was what I did.

Then Brian, her secret crush, had paid all this attention to me. Who could blame him? I was wearing a black slinky number I'd ordered from a posh catalog. But I was more interested in having a friend. I could get a date once I'd locked Candy down.

I'd tried to get Brian to partner with her in this game, but he'd insisted on me.

I studied her expression. Was I about to lose my first line on a friend? I elbowed Brian. "Candy looks hot tonight, doesn't she?" She must've heard me; she tilted her head, a hopeful look on her face. "She's a total babe."

He frowned. "Who? You're the only babe I'm interested in," he slurred.

Shit! "I have a boyfriend," I hastily said. "But I bet I could get Candy's digits for you."

"Your guy's not here, is he?" Brian said. "When the cat's away, the mice will play, right?" He leaned in to kiss me, but I turned my face.

Candy flounced off just as the pong ball plopped into one of our cups. Brian handed the drink to me. "I'll give you the honors since you've got a lot of catching up to do."

"Yeah. Sure thing." I put the cup to my lips.

"Chug, chug!"

AN HOUR OR SO AGO

"I don't feel s'good," I told Brian. My legs didn't want to work right. I hadn't drunk more than three cups of beer, so why was I this weakened?

Was this part of my Arcana transformation? Were more powers coming online?

The room blurred. Faces were fuzzy.

I wanted to find Candy, but Brian had his fist clamped around my left arm and was steering me away from the crowd.

My tongue didn't seem to fit in my mouth as I asked, "Where're we heading?"

"Don't you want to see my room?"

Was it just me or did he sound way less drunk than he had before? "Nooo. Wanna find Candy."

"Your friend's hooking up with somebody else." His grip tightened. "Come on, we want to show you something upstairs."

We? I managed to crane my head around. Three of his teammates had joined us, one of them taking my other arm.

I was the Huntress, but the way these guys looked at me gave me chills. . . . All of a sudden, *I* felt like the prey. "Not going upstairs!" I flung away, using all my strength, but they just laughed.

One of them said, "We caught a wildcat tonight."

I'd tracked wildcats through dense forests. Right now, I was nothing like them. I had as much bite as a newborn kitten.

Realization dawned. These guys . . . they'd *drugged* me.

I'd expected treachery from other Arcana. *Not* from humans.

We passed wasted partiers. I tried to signal for help, but no one paid any attention to me. The four players steered me to another hallway. My stomach dropped when I saw a stairway ahead. I couldn't let them force me up those steps—

Candy! My eyes went wide. She was in the hall making out with some guy! "Candy!" I screamed, but it came out like a slurred murmur.

I tried to reach for her, but those guys had my arms. "Help me!" I had never in all my life said those words.

She drew back from the guy. She would see what was wrong with me! She would *know* what these assholes had done.

She looked me up and down. With a smirk, she muttered, "What a total slut"—then went back to kissing that guy.

Tears pricked my eyes. I wanted to sob. My first friend.

At the foot of the stairs, I attempted a last show of resistance, but only managed to collapse.

Brian caught me, laughing. "Oops-a-daisy!" He wrapped an arm around me, hauling me up against his side. "There she goes." With another laugh, he told the others, "Have you ever noticed they never make it to the stairs?"

They'd drugged other girls too.

My vision grew blurrier as they forced me up the steps. My shoes were gone, my limp feet dragging behind me. I couldn't move my legs, couldn't fight.

Soon I'd black out. Would I remember any of this?

The last thing I saw was the door to Brian's room.

NOW

The four had just decided on dibs—Brian would "go" first—when some other guy barged into the room. He demanded a spot in line, or at least to "film the action" on his phone.

I'd never felt frustration like this! Not in waking life. After my parents had burned to death, I used to dream that I was screaming and not making a sound.

Now I was living that nightmare.

I thought of moonlight streaming through the forest. I pictured my bow, and imagined how I would put an arrow into each of these guys—if I could remember this night. I replayed how it'd felt to run the forest with my growing speed and strength. My aunts had been right about one thing.

I am a goddess.

One foot moved slightly. Then the other.

Brian climbed into the bed. "Such a sweet piece of ass," he told me. "I'm going to pound you so hard you'll feel it for a week."

One of the other players said, "Ah, yeah! Nail that bitch."

Another yelled, "Tap that ass!"

My heart thundered. My eyes darted behind my lids. My right hand clenched.

Brian started hiking up my skirt.

My aunts' words resonated within me like a prayer: *Moonlight is doubt. It is the light of darkness. It is the color of nightmares. You were born to shine in dark times. Be the doom of others.*

My eyes flashed open.

Brian's went wide. "Whoa! This bitch is waking up. Get me that drink!"

More drugs? I opened and closed my fists. The hell that would be happening!

One of them sprang across the room to retrieve a cup, hurrying back with it. Brian shifted out of the way to give the other guy access.

When he lifted my head and forced the rim against my lips, I thrashed my head away.

The Moon was regaining her strength. I would be the color of their nightmares.

My hands shot against his chest, stiff-arming him off the bed.

As I sat up, my skin began to turn red for the first time. They scrambled back, horrified. The guy who'd been filming dropped his phone.

With each second I burned red, I shook off more of the drug's effects. When my body was under *my* control again, I stood and smiled at Brian. "I'm going to pound you so hard you'll feel it—*for the rest of your life.*"

One guy tried to run for the door. I vaulted in front of it. "Ah-ah. No one's going to miss out on their turn with me. You'll have to be carried from this bedroom, just like you carried me in."

Red tinged my skin—and my vision. I struck Brian's face first, putting him to the floor with one blow. Another guy swung a fist, but I caught it, squeezing as I kicked the cameraman.

Without thought, I shifted and pivoted, punched and stomped, my combat training taking over.

These men had targeted me, working together. Now I targeted them, my limbs working together. The moves were effortless, the destruction rewarding. Brian vomited each time I booted his stomach, like I was pushing a Puke Now button. Fun!

I'd been no fan of the Arcana game, but if it brought more of this . . .

Cracking bones. Screams. Pleas for me to stop.

Pleas? "You don't get to beg." *Kick.* "*I* didn't get to say a word." *Punch.*

Too soon they all lay on the floor, broken men. I wasn't even out of breath.

I punted each one in the ballbag so hard I doubted they'd ever be raping anyone again. I crushed that asshole's phone, then spat on Brian's bloody face.

As I exited, I realized I'd be underneath that rapist right now if the game hadn't given me abilities—and if my aunts hadn't trained me to use them.

I'd beaten the piss out of those players; now it was Candy's turn. I listened for her voice, stalking her through the huge party. She had no idea the Huntress was on her trail.

I found her downstairs smoking with a group of girls. Judging by the fuck knots in her hair, she'd already been with that guy from earlier. I yanked her around to face me.

Her jaw dropped. "What are you ... h-how? You were comatose."

"And you left me with those animals? You knew what they planned to do to me! You abandoned me."

Recovering from her surprise, she faked a laugh. "You looked like you were about to have a great time with all of them. Slut."

I tilted my head. "How great of a time will you have without your teeth?"

She frowned at me. "What—"

Wham! I punched her in the mouth, knocking her front teeth out. She shrieked, spraying blood.

I turned toward the door, heading back to my dorm. If this was what friendship and dating offered, I hadn't missed anything. Maybe the game *was* my sole purpose, the one thing that could ease my longing.

I was going to pack up tonight and drive straight through to my aunts'. When I got there, I'd tell them, "I'm going to win the whole fucking game."

THE SUN (XIX)

Solomón Heliodoro, Hail the Glorious Illuminator

"Next to me, everything is shadow."

A.k.a.: El Sol

Powers: Solar embodiment (can emit sunlight from his skin and eyes). Solar manipulation (can burn enemies or strike them with madness and attack with solar winds and flares). Command inducement and sense scrying (can control Bagmen and borrow their senses).

Special Skills: Enhanced charisma, showmanship.

Weapons: Bagmen.

Tableau: A child wrapped in a red pennant is surrounded by sunflowers. Above, the sun blazes down with a menacing face.

Icon: Yellow sun.

Unique Arcana Characteristics: Golden beams radiate from his eyes, and his bronzed skin glows.

Before Flash: Purdue history grad student and part-time rave promoter from Spain.

WEST LAFAYETTE, INDIANA
DAY 0

"Is it just me, or is our sex life improving by the minute?" I asked my two partners as I worked to catch my breath.

Beatrice curled up against my side, her panting exhalations cooling my damp skin. "Not just you."

Joe was sprawled like a starfish, his legs draped over ours. He grunted, "Not just you."

Bea traced a heart over my chest, giving me goose bumps. "If this continues, where will we end up?"

"Let's find out, *querida*." And we would—because I would *never* let either of them go. Bea and I had been great together—I'd fallen for her at first sight—but Joe had been the third piece of our puzzle.

Today was the two-year anniversary of our trio, and I expected a hundred more.

She laughed and sat up, stretching her arms over her head—to my delight. I'd been with her since before Joe, three years or so, but even her simplest movements could still stir me.

"I see that look in your eyes." She raised her brows. "But we have work."

Joe rose up on his elbows. "The Spaniard wants another round? Jesus, he'll kill us before it's all over."

"That so, *cariño*?" I lunged for him, wrestling him till he was begging for mercy.

Bea slipped out of bed and headed for the bathroom, saying over her shoulder, "We're going to be late. It's like I keep saying: something will—"

"—always go sideways," Joe and I finished in unison.

Grumbling, I released him. Everyone thought we had so much fun as party promoters, but hosting raves was a lot of work. Especially since we moved them around from one abandoned building to the next.

Each time, we had to do a fresh setup—power, lights, sound, decorations, etc.—and we had to do it on the day of, else our equipment would get stolen.

We worked like beasts for hours before the rave even started, then pulled an all-nighter alongside the attendees. But we'd almost made enough money to travel over winter break.

When Joe rose from the bed, I watched him stretch with just as much heat as I had Bea. Who would've known?

He caught me leering at him in the mirror and the cocky *cabrón* smirked, so I threw a pillow at him.

He chucked it back. "I don't care what we do after work, but tequila needs to be involved."

Bea peeked out of the doorway. "Seconded."

I nodded. "Motion carried." We wouldn't be together without the help of Cuervo.

Two years ago, Joe had fallen for Bea as hard as I had, trying to steal her from me, which had brought about the worst—and the best—day of my life.

Worst? Bea's heart had been so torn between her boyfriend and her determined new suitor that she'd threatened to cut us both out of her life. I'd decided to fight him. Then I'd realized Joe—a linebacker in his undergraduate years—was a really big fucker who could probably kick even my ass.

Best? After some tequila, I'd muttered that she deserved to have us both. I'd been half-joking, but she'd agreed, telling us we could share her in and out of bed or never see her again!

Which left me and Joe to figure out the rest. Our love for Bea—and more tequila—got the three of us into bed together. To our surprise, it'd been *amazing*.

Life-altering.

I couldn't survive without them both. I'd bought two rings. Tonight after work, I would ask them to marry me.

Our Roll into Classes Rave had been a blowout last year. Students had stayed up and gone to class still rolling.

We were hosting this year's version—"Haunted Asylum"—in the basement of an abandoned mental ward outside of town, and expected an even larger turnout. As Joe had said, "Dude, the acoustics down here are sick." After a few hiccups, he was turning into an excellent DJ.

For hours, we worked our asses off to prep the place. Sundown found us sweating, grimy, and sore, but in good spirits. By the light of our staging lamps, Joe was stacking a huge bank of speakers, while Bea organized the cash till and wristbands. I was securing one of the last lighting units to my effects truss.

During setup, Joe and Bea took care of the "guts," and I perfected the "skin." I was in charge of all the design effects, but rave lighting was my passion. From my console, I could control the focus, color, and intensity of the moving beams to amplify the energy of the music and manipulate the attendees' emotions. Joe and Bea made fun of me, saying I got high on the power.

Now Joe rolled his head on his neck. "I'm finished with my rig."

Bea said, "Other than trash cleanup, I'm set too."

Joe squeezed my shoulder. "You need help, Spaniard?"

"I can fit two more light sets along this truss." It would direct the focus to him. "Could you guys go grab them from the van?"

"We're on it," Joe said. He took Bea's hand, and they headed up the stairs.

The three of us worked together seamlessly. Though I always forgot the cordless drill battery, Bea never failed to bring a backup. Joe made sure we drank enough Gatorade to stay hydrated for the long night ahead. I kept everyone on an even keel whenever something went sideways.

Bea was right; it always did.

I took off my shirt and wiped my face, surveying the area. We'd transformed the basement into a spooky rave paradise.

Drawing on first-hand accounts and grainy pics—I'd eagerly researched the gruesome history of this place—I'd painted rusted cell doors and bloody examination curtains. I'd dressed mannequins in gore-stained straightjackets (thanks, eBay). Bea, Joe, and I had spattered lab coats to wear as well.

In the promotion biz, presentation was everything.

I was beaming I was so proud of them. Of *us.*

Suddenly, a breeze gusted inside the area, scattering our trash pile of boxes and wrappers. I scratched my head. No way a wind could reach this basement, and it was too strong to be a draft.

Before I could determine the source of the wind, vertigo seized me. The room seemed to be spinning. No, *I* was spinning! Yet at the same time some kind of weight pressed down on my body.

What the hell is happening to me?

I felt like gravity affected me more than ever before! Pressure made my legs buckle. I went to my knees, my panicked gaze darting. That wind increased and grew hot, spiraling around me. The spinning sensation intensified. Any more, and I'd lose consciousness.

I tried to call for Joe and Bea. They were still outside, would never hear me down here. What was taking them so long?

Spinning, spinning. Blackness was about to overwhelm me! My eyes slid closed, and gravity made my body collapse. . . .

I woke on the floor in the basement, in total confusion—and darkness.

Our staging lamps weren't on? The generator must've conked out. A chill skittered up my spine. Then how *long* had I been unconscious? I called, "Bea? Joe?" No answer. I tentatively sat up. "*Por Dios,* my head!" It was splitting.

I must've had some kind of aneurism or something. What else could explain my hallucinations from earlier, my collapse? "Where are you guys?" Yelling magnified the pain in my skull, but I didn't care.

"Answer me. . . ." I trailed off when I heard footsteps in the stairwell. "Guys?" A soft wail sounded in the darkness. Then a deeper one. "Who's there?"

Fear made my heart thunder, my pulse racing. I would give anything to see! "Who's down here?" *In the dark basement with me.*

Some light kicked on, faint at first, then growing stronger. I glanced behind me, trying to find the source—then frowned down at my chest. Lost my breath. *"Qué coño es esto?"* What the fuck is that?

My flesh . . . it *glowed.* I was giving off more light than our staging lamps would. My skin grew brighter and brighter.

I craned my head up, lost my breath. Looming over me were two . . . *monstruos!*

Monsters with weathered and creased faces. Cracked lips. Pale eyes running with pus.

Why were those creatures wearing Bea and Joe's clothes? "I-Is this a prank?" I gazed from one to the other, disbelieving my eyes. These things were Joe and Bea! *"Cariño? Querida?"* Bea's filmy gaze focused on my neck. No, my *throat*—

Joe lunged for me, sending me flying. "What the hell are you *doing?*" I smacked the ground, the force stealing my breath.

He leapt atop me; I thrashed, shoving against his big chest. He snared one of my flailing arms. His teeth sank into my skin!

I yelled from the pain. "Joe, why . . . what???" He was sucking my blood!

Bea dropped to her knees and joined him, seizing and biting my other arm.

"*Ahh!* Why are you . . . you can't . . ." They were *drinking* me!

My cordless drill lay on the ground nearby. If I could free one of my arms, I could snag it and bash Bea's head, then use it on Joe.

No! Everything in me rebelled. I'd rather die than harm them. "Please don't make me hurt you!" *Please stop biting!*

Both of them stopped, releasing my skin. *Let me go!* They dropped my arms.

I scuttled back, thinking, *Get away from me, get away.* They rose and backed up several steps, their movements almost robotic. As I dragged myself to my feet, they just stood there, swaying slightly in unison. Was I somehow controlling them? Mentally?

I pictured them walking a step back, then a step forward.

They did the same.

I *was* controlling them! Why was this happening to us? This whole situation seemed supernatural, but I didn't believe in hocus-pocus bullshit. Maybe they'd been bitten by something rabid down here, a bat or something.

So why was I still glowing?

"I-I'm going to get you to a hospital." Tears welled in my eyes. "Doctors will make you better." Then I pictured how others would react to my girlfriend and boyfriend.

Their skin was leathery. Those pale eyes were blank. My blood stained each one's cracked lips and chin.

The two looked like . . . bloodthirsty zombies. Like I might dress them in costume. But this was *real*. Right?

Steps sounded in the stairwell once more. More of the leather-faced creatures shuffled inside. Something outside had *turned* them. Had turned my Bea and Joe.

Into zombies.

I was in an insane asylum. And maybe I belonged here. . . .

JUDGMENT (XX)

Gabriel Arendgast, the Archangel

"I watch you like a hawk."

A.k.a.: The Seventh Coming, the Guardian Angel, Exalted One, Gabriel of the Light

Powers: Flight, supernatural senses, speed, strength, healing, tracking, and endurance.

Special Skills: Enhanced aiming, swordsmanship.

Weapons: In past games, he wielded the Sword of Right, but it was stolen.

Tableau: An archangel carrying a sword, flying over a mass of bodies.

Icon: A pair of wings.

Unique Arcana Characteristics: Large black wings, talon-tipped fingers. Outdated speech and old-fashioned clothing.

Before Flash: Prophesied to be the reincarnation of the great *Arendgast*—an errand spirit (more commonly known as an angel). Worshipped by the Sect of Arendgast, a remote, ages-old cult, separated from modern society.

THE MOUNT ON HIGH
CANADIAN WILDS
DAY O

"Are you ready to begin, Exalted One?" the high sectaire asked me, his bushy gray brows raised.

"Yes." I removed my suit coat, laying it on my bed, then untied my cravat. "I am ready," I lied. What man of nineteen would be ready for a day like this?

My tone was even despite the dread that threatened to overwhelm me. After removing my vest and fob watch, I drew off my white lawn shirt, taking my time to fold it, my gaze surveying my lantern-lit room, possibly for the last time.

My chambers were the most luxurious in the colony, my bed large enough for half a dozen people. I had countless stacks of books—my only link to the outside world—but they were all ancient. Above my desk was artwork depicting angels falling from the heavens.

Was I about to join them?

I could stall no longer. I straightened and headed toward my door, exiting before the high sectaire. We made our way down the corridor toward the great cavern chamber.

Centuries ago, the sect—chased from Europe, and then from the very ground itself—had moved to this secluded mountain, seeking refuge inside the heart of its peak.

In the cavern chamber, dozens of sectaires had gathered to follow my historic walk. All told, this colony numbered seventy-eight, the number of cards in a Tarot deck. Half were female, half male. Their voices rang with excitement. The sect had awaited this moment for generations.

As we entered, an elder called, "Quiet everyone."

At the candlelit altar, I stood beside the high sectaire, making my face impassive. No one would ever know the strangling urge I had to flee. I was about to start sweating, despite my lack of a shirt. I resisted the impulse to rub my damp palms on my trousers.

In a resonant voice, the man addressed everyone, signaling the beginning of today's ritual. I barely registered his words as I contemplated my life.

As ever, I wondered about my birth parents. I'd been missing for seventeen years. Did they still long for me as I longed for them? They would never know the importance of their sacrifice. Could they have accepted the ritual I was about to take part in?

I doubted they could have accepted my dual nature.

An Arendgast was both angel and animal, a creature torn between base and noble instincts. When I'd been twelve, I'd asked the high sectaire how I could overcome my animal instinct for self-preservation during the ritual. His answer had filled me with horror.

Perhaps I should have run then. . . .

Though our records—the Chronicles of Arendgast—had been burned long ago by fearful villagers, the elders had passed down sacred knowledge to help me in the Arcana game, tales of the past and foretellings of the future.

I was to beware my worst enemies: Death, the Empress, and the Emperor. My staunch ally was forever the Tower; I was to seek him out as soon as possible.

I had also been prophesied in this game to give my heart to a great warrior, another Arcana: "One who slays from afar."

Surely that meant I would survive the ritual!

The elders had also passed down the date of the foretold Great Cataclysm.

Today.

The apocalypse would befall us, the game beginning in its wake. But I should have heard Arcana calls by now. What if the elders had misremembered the date?

The lack of calls meant one of two things, both of them dire: I was not the Arendgast. Or the game didn't begin today.

Either option equaled my demise.

My life had taken just one fateful turn to get me to this precipice, figuratively and literally. When I'd been two, a sectaire—allegedly a minor arcana—believed he'd witnessed the earliest seed of my tableau flickering over me. That night, he'd stolen me from my birth parents, bringing me back to the Mount.

I gazed over the crowd, finding him. His face was red, his eyes bleary. Had he truly seen my tableau so long ago? He swore I was the seventh coming of Gabriel.

But then, that sectaire also drank a lot.

And right now he looked . . . nervous.

My entire destiny had been shaped by a drunken sectaire. Would I pay the ultimate price for another man's mistake?

"Exalted One . . . ?"

I snapped my gaze to the high sectaire. "I am ready," I lied again. Though I'd spent my life preparing for this, I was most decidedly *not* ready to free fall a mile to the ground.

If I made the leap of faith too far in advance of the game, my wings wouldn't be fully formed.

The others parted the way for me to reach the ledge. As I trudged through the cavern, sectaires tried to catch my eye for tonight's closing ritual, reaching out to touch my chest and back. *"Choose me,"* they whispered.

Was I the only one who doubted my survival? Each step brought me closer to my probable death.

I swallowed when the edge of the cliff came into view, but I kept walking.

Closer.

If I was the Archangel and the game truly began today, my wings and claws would burst from my skin as I fell. My senses and healing would be heightened.

I would fly over lands I didn't know, loosed from the Mount for the first time.

Closer.

As the sun set, I would return with fire, a ceremonial light, all part of the ritual. Then the colony would drink strong spirits and celebrate into the night, the great cavern ringing with cheer.

I would be expected to choose four bedmates among the sectaires, the most beautiful and handsome among them. Having never so much as kissed, I was nearly as nervous about that part as I was about the fall!

Gods, I'd never wanted to live more.

Closer.

I emerged from under the rock overhang, blinking my eyes against the sun.

Closer. *What if they had the date wrong?*

The brilliant skies were cloudless. Far above, an aeroplane—one of those mysterious crafts!—crossed the blue expanse. Hardly an apocalyptic day.

Closer . . . Here. At the cliffside, I gazed down at the jagged snow-covered rocks below, fear choking me. My heart thundered as I replayed the high sectaire's answer to my query all those years ago: "'Tis our duty to ensure you become the Archangel. Should your instinct for self-preservation overcome you, we shall see to it that you leap."

In other words, all of the sectaires at my back would push me.

My fate was fixed; somehow I would leave this ledge. Would I do so proudly or with shame? As soon as the high sectaire signaled, I would go quickly. Before I lost my nerve. Fists clenched, I inhaled quick bursts of air, biting back yells of terror.

He turned to me. "Whenever you are r—"

I stepped off into nothing.

The air shrilled over my ears. My long hair whipped around my face.

Falling . . .

Falling!

Nothing had happened! Which meant I was *dying*—

Pain!

Stabbing agony spread over my back. *Can't breathe. Barely conscious.* I must've landed, breaking on the rocks.

So why was I still falling?

PAIN.

I raised my hands in front of my face, gnashing my teeth as talons burst from my fingertips! Disbelieving, I craned my head from side to side—silky blackness fluttered behind me. Wings! I concentrated on expanding them—using them to *survive.*

The ground rushed ever closer.

I tried flapping my new wings. Swooping? Flying in general?? None of the elders had passed down practical tips on flight!

New muscles in my back contracted. My wings extended, shocking me with their size! With all my might, I strained my new muscles—

My wings caught the air; my body jerked as if I'd jumped with a tether attached to me.

Too much pressure! *"Ahhhh!"* The bones would surely snap. Heart about to explode, I let instinct take over. Without thinking, I maneuvered into a dive.

As I shot headfirst through the sky, my wings seemed to act on their own. They dug into the air like paddles in water, propelling me forward. And again. My speed remained constant, but now I was flying parallel to the ground.

I was ... *flying.*

The pain from before gave way to euphoria. All my life, I'd waited to soar!

And my senses! I heard ice cracking in a distant glacier, and the cries of jubilant sectaires all the way up at the Mount. Far to the north I spied a white arctic hare, huddled down amid miles of snow. The sight of prey affected me; my talons extended even more from my altered fingertips.

Euphoria. Ecstasy. Air slipped over my wings like a caress from heaven.

As I glided, I blinked at a shadow sliding over the snow below me. Black on white. Fearsome, bold.

My lips parted. That terrifying shadow was . . . mine.

The image was forever burned into my mind; a reminder of why I had grown these wings.

To kill.

THE WORLD (XXI)

Tess Quinn, This Unearthly One

"Trapped in the palm of my hand."

A.k.a.: Quintessence, Miracle

Powers: Levitation, teleportation, astral projection, time manipulation, intangibility, Arcana visitation.

Special Skills: Spying.

Weapons: A wooden staff.

Tableau: A bare-chested maiden with a swath of white cloth around her hips, framed by symbols of the four elements.

Icon: A globe.

Unique Arcana Characteristics: When the World utilizes her powers, her reactorlike body quickly burns calories. Inefficient use of her abilities will result in sudden, massive weight loss.

Before Flash: Honors high school student and service award recipient.

BROKEN BOW, OKLAHOMA
DAY 0

I'll die before I ever get my first kiss.

I sprawled on my bed, biting my nails, miserable. Here I was, sweet seventeen (going on eighteen) and never been kissed. How pitiful was that?

I had all these new abilities, but I'd kill for a kiss. And once I got it, I'd hit the *play* button for my life. Things might actually start to happen for me—exciting things.

My phone rang. Expecting one of the fussbudgety officers of my service club, I sighed, taking my time to roll over and answer.

I blinked at the caller ID: "T-Tony Trovato?" Was calling *me*? I had the hugest crush on him. I started to do my usual anxiety trembling, only this time I began to float upward—without even touching my staff.

Tony T. was Sicilian but also a punk skateboarder, like a supercute hybrid. He wasn't the guy every girl in school wanted.

Only the *smart* girls.

I cleared my throat to answer, but he'd already hung up. *Nooo!* I slowly drifted back down to sit on the bed. "Why would he call me?" I asked my empty room. For tutoring. Surely.

I wished I could see him right now. Did he have his books cracked open? Was he panicking about class tomorrow?

I glanced at the staff on my bed. I could astral-project to him and see what he was up to. . . .

No, Tess. Don't you do it. Spying was wrong.

When I'd found that beat-up old staff in Gramps's attic and discovered my abilities, I'd realized I was a superhero. I wanted to be a *good* one. So I'd outlined rules.

1) *Don't use powers unless absolutely necessary.* This was tough because I liked myself whenever I was actively using them. I felt confident and witty.

Not that anyone could see or hear me.

2) *Don't spy.* Even tougher.

3) *Don't tell parents.* To convince them of my powers, I'd have to demonstrate; Dad might legit have a heart attack.

4) *Don't rob banks.*

I was rethinking my last rule. My parents were closing in on retirement age, but they were strapped. Dad still worked two jobs. Nineteen years ago they'd spent a fortune on assisted reproduction to have me—their little miracle—and still hadn't caught up.

They'd given up everything just to bring me into the world.

I gazed at my phone. Maybe I could bend my rules in case of an emergency—like finding out why Tony had called! I'd only go to him for a second, sneak a peek, then project myself right back home.

I couldn't go for much longer anyway. I'd discovered the hard way that each astral projection, levitation, and teleportation burned fat, leaving my body skeletal. I'd plump back up again once I'd scarfed down a few thousand calories, but I didn't want to find out my limit on fat loss.

I set the phone away and laid my hands on the staff. Though it didn't look like much, energy thrummed through it.

I didn't look like much either, but my powers were unreal. Last week, I'd dreamed I was at one with the ether, just an atom among atoms, and I'd gone freaking intangible! I'd floated through my bed, through the floor, and down into the kitchen. Thank goodness my parents hadn't been there.

Closing my eyes, I imagined myself near Tony. Like a shot, I projected to a room. *His* room? I came to rest horizontally—right above his bed.

His face was, like, six feet below mine! He was shirtless, lying with the comforter at his waist. No books were open. He was texting someone. Or trying to. He typed, erased, then typed again.

Then he tossed the phone away, and threw his arm over his face, like he felt hopeless. Could he possibly have been nervous about texting *me*?

Yeah, right, Tess.

He reached for his laptop, then clicked a key. His one-click pulled up . . .

My picture.

Tony liked me! Me, me, me!

Then I frowned. That picture had accompanied an article about the service organization I'd started, and I'd always thought the pic made me look hella fat. When that article ran, I'd cried in front of a mirror, calling myself Fatty MacFatterson. I'd just *known* that everyone else at school had called me that as well.

Had I been totally off base? Tony was looking at that image with his brows drawn—like he was in LOVE!

I could've stayed there sighing over his expression for days, but I needed to get back, would burn too many calories if I lingered. My parents already suspected I was bulimic. I knew this because I'd spied— *spying is wrong*—on them.

The first time I'd levitated, I'd been delighted to lose all my baby fat. Then I'd realized how important every pound was. Every single calorie counted. Something had to fuel my unreal powers. . . .

One of Tony's hands started rubbing down his belly.

My eyes went wide. *No. Way.*

Spying is wrong, spying is wrong, SPYING IS WRONG!

His hand dipped lower and lower. The comforter shifted and revealed his navel. How could a navel be so cute? And sexy?

I was pretty sure I was in love with Tony forever.

Or in lust.

I was now DYING for my first kiss. Tomorrow I would march up to him at school and press my lips to his. My new life as a superhero and Tony's girlfriend could finally get started.

His lips *were* the play button to start up a new chapter. Considering his reaction to my photo, we might even . . . have sex.

When his hand reached its destination, I nearly whimpered with embarrassment and excitement. But somehow I closed my eyes and forced myself to return home.

I opened my eyes, then frowned. Not home? My new surroundings were sort of gauzy and undefined. Everything around me looked blurry, like stuff sometimes did when I dreamed.

I glanced around. A hot guy was standing not ten feet from me, wearing broken-in jeans and no shirt. *Well, hellooooo there.* He had ripped muscles like no tomorrow and smooth dark skin—except for some wicked scars on his chest. He should have to carry a permit for cheekbones that fine!

I wanted to see his eyes, but they were squeezed shut.

"Howdy," I said. When I was projecting like this, there was no time for shyness.

His gaze snapped to my face. "Who are you? How are you . . . *here?*"

"I might be dreaming. Or I might have astral-projected. Who can tell? Cool accent, by the way. Where are you from?"

In a stunned tone, he grated, "Africa." Were those ripped muscles straining? "We are Kenyan."

We? I dug through some of the mysterious ether to get closer, then glanced past him. He was hand in hand with a young woman, whose eyes remained closed as she murmured in a low tone. Of course he'd be taken. A little nightie showed off her gorgeous figure. When I gazed at her model-perfect face, I felt a rash starting on my elbow.

I scratched awkwardly. "Uh, I'm from Broken Bow." As if they would've heard of that. "It's the gateway to Beavers Bend," I said, jabbering on. "Which probably isn't an internationally recognized destination, unless one were a beaver, because then it's, like, *the* place—"

"Do you not see the lights?" he demanded, raising his gaze to the sky.

I squinted. "Lights?" I could kind of make out something that resembled a laser light show crossed with aurora borealis. "I'm not really there."

"You are a ghost as well?" His voice was getting weaker.

Ghost? "Do you mean intangible? I guess I can be a ghost. Well, not on purpose."

"Can you help us? We are . . . we are being *killed right now!*"

My eyes went wide. "Wh-what are you talking about?"

"The lights! The flames! If I can't remain . . . a ghost . . . we will burn."

No wonder he was straining! I sputtered, "How can I help? Can you teleport?" It took me a ton of calories just to teleport myself; I couldn't imagine doing it with someone else.

He murmured, "Teleport?" as if he was chewing over the idea, considering it. "I do not know."

"I want to help you!" But I felt myself fading from this place. "Do you have a wooden staff? Can you eat something?"

"Eat? *Eat?*" He shook his head at me. "Beware the lights and the roar, child." Then he drew that woman against him, enfolding her in his arms.

Though I fought to stay with them, I couldn't. As I disappeared from the ether, I was still calling, "Let me help!"

I woke, blinking in confusion. What a freaky dream! Wait, where was I now? "Ugh." I was floating, my face mashed against my bedroom ceiling. Great, I'd drooled on it again.

I concentrated on grounding my feet. But when I maneuvered my body from horizontal to vertical, my sweats slipped clean off.

Oh, no. I must've lost ten, maybe even twenty pounds! Outside, the sun had set—my parents were going to be home any minute now!

All the girls at school were so concerned with losing weight. I *needed* it. I yanked up my sweats, cinching the tie tight, then weakly hobbled down the stairs to the kitchen.

I hit the fridge first, assessing the contents. I guzzled a gallon of whole milk, then a quart of flavored coffee creamer (my mom's favorite, but desperate times). Then I noshed my way through a package of cookie dough.

The pantry was next. I choked down a jar of peanut butter—no time for a spoon; I scooped it out with my fingers. Then I popped open a can of macadamia nuts, tucked the rim against my mouth, and tipped the can up, gobbling down its contents.

Potato chips. More peanut butter. An entire blueberry pie (Dad's favorite). A pint of ice cream. A six-pack of my parents' Ensure.

Slowly my body took on flesh again. *Need more....*

I was microwaving a frozen lasagna while inhaling another pint of ice cream when my parents walked in.

Dad murmured, "What the ...?"

My goopy fingers hovered at my mouth. I gazed around, seeing the scene from their eyes. All the cabinet doors were open. The refrigerator too. Empty jars and bottles were strewn all over the kitchen. Milk spattered the floor and the front of my T-shirt.

Eyes watering, Mom sank into a chair at the kitchen table. "Tess, we're going to get you help." She removed her glasses to dab at her tears.

Dad stood behind her, his hands on her shoulders. "Tomorrow we're taking you to a facility for teens with eating problems."

No, no. I had to be in school tomorrow. I was going to get my first kiss! "I don't have an eating problem." I swiped my face with the back of my hand. Chocolate, peanut butter, and blueberry came away.

"It's perfectly natural to deny it, honey," Mom said. "They told us you would. You're just going to have to trust us."

Dad's eyes grew misty too. "Miracle, we love you. You know you're our entire world. We can get through anything together."

Past Mom and Dad, movement caught my attention. Lights were flickering in the night sky.

I frowned. Were those the kind of burning lights the Kenyan had faced? *Beware the lights.* I dropped the ice cream on the floor. "Mom, Dad, we need to get into the tornado shelter. Now!"

"What are you talking about, Tess?" Dad asked, turning to follow my gaze toward the window. "You guys, just look at that!" He sounded hypnotized. "It's the aurora borealis."

Mom stood and turned. "My word, it's spectacular!"

As if in a trance, they headed toward the foyer.

"No!" I rushed after them, but slipped in food, face-planting. "Oomph! W-wait . . ." I sucked in a breath. "The lights are dangerous! We have to get in the shelter!"

As I scrambled up, I heard the front door open. By the time I'd caught up to them, they were standing outside, transfixed.

I kept my gaze down, afraid I'd be mesmerized too. "Please come back inside with me!" Some kind of roar sounded. The Kenyan had warned of that too. Surely this was a twister coming?

I grabbed my parents' arms, yanking on them, but I was weak, still exhausted from using my powers. My folks didn't budge. "Please, I am begging you to come with me!"

The air kept getting hotter. I dared a glance up—just to the horizon. Over the plains came another kind of light, as if the sun were rising. My parents didn't see it, were too hypnotized by the aurora.

Rays blazed, then . . . a giant ball of flames seared everything in its reach—and it was heading for us!

Armageddon. It had to be.

Tears welled at the sight; I shook worse than I ever had. "Mommy! Daddy! P-please." The fire hurtled toward us, but they wouldn't move.

No time to get them to safety.

Could I teleport with my parents? Or go intangible with them, like the Kenyan had with that woman?

I forced myself to close my eyes—though the freaking apocalypse was bearing down on us!—and concentrated on picturing my staff. Then I imagined the three of us were atoms among other atoms, just floating around in the ether.

I opened my eyes. My parents were in that blurry place with me! I glanced past them—the wave of burning light was about to hit! Mom screamed. Dad tried to shield us.

I cried out when it passed through us. The house was an instant inferno, windows shattering. The wave was so vast, we were still engulfed in fire.

We needed to get underground, to the shelter! I imagined us tele-porting there. Teleporting . . . traversing . . . crossing physical space . . .

Nothing.

Mom craned her head around, asking me, "Wh-what's happening?"

Dad turned to me, rasping, "Did we die, Miracle?"

I shook my head. "I'm trying . . . to keep you safe." Nobody would be dying if I had anything to say about it!

"Keep us safe? Oh, honey"—he sounded horrified—"you're so *thin*!"

I peeked at my arms. They were like sticks. I only had so much fat stored.

Mom gasped. "Why are you losing weight? Whatever you're doing—stop!"

"Nooo!" I was about to wither away. If they would be incinerated, I'd die with them.

Dad glanced from my face to my hand on his arm. He must've felt the power, must've realized I was fueling it. He murmured, "I love you both." Then he yanked away from me.

His body disappeared. A pile of ash grew at our feet. He'd become . . . nothing.

Mom and I screamed. My body recoiled as if I'd almost teleported. For her, I tried to again. Carrying only one, I was so close . . . almost . . .

Ah, God, can't.

I clung to her arm as she knelt and reached for Dad's ashes. She gazed up and said, "Let me go. Tess, *live*."

I gritted my teeth, shaking my head.

"Love you so much." With a watery smile, she peeled my fingers off her arm. One by one . . .

THE EMPRESS (III)

Evangeline "Evie" Greene, Our Lady of Thorns

"Come, touch . . . but you'll pay a price."

A.k.a.: The Poison Princess, Phyta, the May Queen, the Queen of Thorns, Mistress of Flora, Lady Lotus. *Sievā* (to Death) and *peekôn* (to Jack).

Powers: Can create, shape, and control plants and trees. Can deliver poisons through her claws and lips, and spores from her hair and hands. Chlorokinetic scrying (can perceive through plants). Regeneration.

Special Skills: Mesmerizing.

Weapons: Plants, trees, poisonous spores, thorn tornados.

Tableau: A woman sitting upon a throne with her arms open wide, wearing a poppy-red gown and a crown with twelve stars; her hair is strewn with poppies, vines, and strands of red. White roses surround her throne, and the rolling hills behind her are awash in green and red—from both crops and blood.

Icon: White rose.

Unique Arcana Characteristics: Hair turns red, and fingernails morph into thorn claws. Glyphs on her skin glow from green to gold, each one representing a weapon in her arsenal

Before Flash: A cheerleader at Sterling High in Louisiana. The night before Day 0, her sixteenth birthday party was broken up by the sheriff's department.

STERLING, LOUISIANA
DAY 0

When I hadn't heard from Mel or Brandon by noon, panic set in. Why wouldn't they pick up their phones?

Surely the two of them hadn't gotten . . . gaffled.

Especially when no one else seemed to have been arrested. Without my cell, I'd been on my laptop, scouring students' social media for info.

All morning, I'd looked at keg-party pics and Solo-cup shares. I'd read updates from kids bragging about being at the party of the year.

Not a word about the cops. And apparently, Mom hadn't heard anything either. . . .

I'd woken at dawn in the middle of the cane field, having slept soundly for hours. Surprisingly, I hadn't been hungover—a miracle considering how tanked I'd been, so drunk I'd hallucinated worse than ever before.

Though desperate to shower and brush my teeth, I hadn't wanted Mom to see me in the clothes I'd gone out in. After a while, I hadn't cared.

She'd been so distracted by the drought, on the phone with another farmer, that she hadn't even noticed I was wearing a Versace halter and a moth-eaten pair of last year's jodhpurs.

Mom would've heard about the bust by then, yet she'd said nothing, just absently kissed my cheek before running off to another emergency farmers' meeting.

After I'd showered and dressed, I'd begun to feel confident that my boyfriend had truly hushed the situation.

Just as he'd said he would. My drunken knight in shining armor had won his battle.

Now I patted the enormous diamond solitaire around my neck, realizing that Brandon Radcliffe was not just the type of boy I needed in my life; he was the one I *wanted*—dependable, happy-go-lucky, easy to read.

Not brooding, mysterious, and impossible to decipher.

I decided to get something locked down with my boyfriend, so I'd stop thinking stupid thoughts about Angola-bound Cajuns.

With that in mind, I called Brandon's cell from my home line yet again, intending to leave a message this time.

"Hey, Brand, I hope everything's okay. Starting to worry." I nibbled my bottom lip, debating how to begin this. "Last night, about our conversation . . . we got interrupted—when you went off to save the day for me. And I just wanted to tell you my decision."

I paused, knowing there was no turning back from this. "My decision is . . . yes. I'll spend the night with you next weekend." *Done. Locked down.* "I . . . I'm . . ." Relieved? Nervous? "Um, call me. At home."

He still hadn't called by three in the afternoon, when Mel sauntered into my room.

"Where in the hell have you been?" My mood was *foul.* My plans to talk to Gran had been thwarted. I hadn't dared to risk Mom's anger—or worse—to call Gran from the house phone. "What happened to you last night?"

"Spencer and I went to his car, totally hooked up. I threw one over on him, released some steam, and he's puppy-dog whipped now." She made a whip-cracking sound. "Melly's got mojo—he wants an ER."

Exclusive relationship? Already? I felt excitement for her, before remembering I was pissed.

"Just when we were finishing up, the cops came," Mel said. "We drove out the back way."

"Why didn't you come here to find me?" I demanded.

She blinked. "I just did. So what happened to you, Eves?"

"Hmm. After Brandon left to go smooth things over with the sheriff and *find you*, I sat alone in the woods." *I was attacked by imaginary enemies and terrified.* "Eventually, I walked miles to get home—with that annoying Jackson Deveaux—and spent the night in the barn." Or rather, in the cane field. "You just left me out there, Mel. You chose bros over hoes," I said, drawing blood.

She gasped. "I thought you were with Brandon! I'll break up with Spencer as penance!"

The thing about Mel—she truly would. How could I stay mad at her when I'd been lying to her so much? In the end, I muttered, "You're forgiven."

"Thank you, Greene! I didn't want to bwake Spencey's wittle heart." She lay back on my bed, adding mischievously, "Not *yet*."

My laptop chimed. "An e-mail from Brandon?" Strange. We texted 99 percent of the time. He basically used his cell phone as his computer.

Everything's cool w/ the cops. Bout to get lecture from Dad tho. Talk later.

"That's weird. Why didn't he just text? He doesn't know that I got stranded without my phone." And why hadn't he even mentioned my voice mail?

"He couldn't text you," Mel said, raising her hands in the air to study her nails. "Everybody's phones got stolen."

"What?" I shot to my feet.

"Why do you think I didn't call all morning?" She rose with a frown. "Somebody snatched wallets and cells right off of people. And they broke into all our cars. But don't worry, your bag didn't get taken."

I bolted out of my room, scrambling down the stairs to reach Mel's Beamer. *My journal!*

"What's wrong with you, Evie?" she demanded, trotting behind me, easily keeping up.

When I got to her car, I frantically slapped the door until she clicked it open. "Jesus, Evie, *chill.*"

My hand trembled as I reached for my bag. Surely a thief wouldn't leave it but then steal the journal. *Please let my drawings be inside!*

I reeled on my feet.

My sketchbook was . . . gone. The one filled with rats and serpents under an apocalyptic sky, bodies mangled in thorn barbed wire, and horrific sack-faced bogeymen. I'd drawn one lapping blood from a victim's throat. Like an animal at a trough.

My tear-blotted drawing of Death on a pale horse was dated from just a couple of nights ago.

It was the journal that Jackson had repeatedly angled to see. My eyes shot wide. The figure skulking among the cars last night—it was *Lionel*, Jackson's best friend.

Lionel had stolen the phones *and* my sketchbook: my very own one-way ticket back to the mental ward at CLC.

And Jackson had kept me occupied, almost kissing me . . . so that Lionel . . .

Oh my God.

Struggling not to throw up, I told Mel, "I know who's got our phones. And if you help me, I'm going to get them back."

"You've had better ideas," Mel muttered, squinting to see out of her bug-splattered windshield. At dusk the insects swarmed, and their squashed bodies had meshed till they were like tar on the glass.

"Maybe so, but I have to do this." I'd never been so angry in all my life, and I'd be damned if I let Jackson get away with this. "Can't you go any faster?"

The sun would set soon, and we hadn't even made the parish levee yet. It'd taken us hours to find the Cajun's address, and then I'd wasted even more time persuading Mel to drive me into the Basin.

"You're lucky I'm in for this one at all, Greene. I'm not losing my license because of a fifth ticket this year. . . ."

She still hadn't stopped grumbling by the time the towering levee loomed. "Let's just call the cops."

And then they'd confiscate my journal. "Jackson only did this because he's a bully and because he *can*. No one ever calls him out. But it's time somebody did."

"How do you know he'll have the phones? You said he just served as a lookout."

I hadn't told Mel exactly how good Jackson had been at his job, only that he'd kept me talking to him while Lionel snatched our things. "I just know, okay?" Which wasn't precisely true. He might not have the phones, but he'd have that sketchbook, which was my main priority.

Not that the phones weren't a big deal. Though I code-locked mine—good luck accessing any of my info—Brandon never locked his phone. And he had all our private texts over the last seven months, not to mention a folder filled with countless pics and vids of me.

Were those Cajuns even now ogling images of me in my bathing suit, or snickering over the goofy faces I'd made for Brand's camera? The corny jokes I'd told?

Had they listened to my voice message from earlier? *"Yes, I'll spend the night with you."* My face burned, my fury ratcheting up to new heights.

When we came upon the new bridge, stretching over acres of swamp, my lips thinned. Without this line of dull gray cement, I'd never even have *known* Jackson Deveaux.

Once we reached the end of the bridge, we were officially in a new parish. Cajun country. Bayou inlets and smaller drawbridges abounded. A pair of wildlife agents in their black trucks sat chatting on a shoulder.

Mel exhaled. "Why are you forcing me into the voice-of-reason role? You know that never works out for us."

"I need to do this," I said simply. When I'd realized Jackson had played me, that the almost-kiss had been a ruse—it'd hurt. Even though I'd never wanted his kiss to begin with.

Why did he have to act as if he'd liked me? It was a mean-spirited, coldhearted prank. How he and Lionel must have laughed at my gullibility!

"It's getting really dark," Mel said as we approached the Basin turnoff. She didn't just mean daylight-wise.

Ominous clouds were back-building over the swamp. "Yeah, but what are the odds that it'll actually rain?" Those clouds reminded me of the scene I'd painted on my wall, and of the blazing eyes I'd soon see.

Folks didn't usually drive to lower land when faced with a gale like that. I didn't know which storm would prove worse—the weather or Jackson's anger.

Didn't matter; I was bent on seeing this through tonight. I directed Mel to turn onto the dirt road that led to the Basin.

After a few miles, she said, "We're not in Kansas anymore."

We saw shrimp boats, bayou shacks, and shipyards filled with rusted heaps. Statuettes of the Virgin Mary graced every other yard. I'd known how Catholic the Basin folk were, but even I was surprised.

We neared the end of the road, closing in on Jackson's address. There were fewer structures down here, but more palmettos, banana trees, cypress. Trash had collected all around the ditch lilies.

By the time the marsh was visible, it was dark and the car lights had come on. Red eyes glowed back from the reeds. Gators. They were so thick, some of the smaller ones lay on top of the others.

Pairs of beady red dots, stacked like ladder rungs.

Mel nervously adjusted her hands on the wheel, but she drove onward. The car crept deeper under a canopy of intertwined limbs and vines, like a ride going into a haunted tunnel.

When the road surrendered to a rutted trail, Jackson's home came into view—a shotgun house, long and narrow, with entrances on both ends. The clapboard framing was a mess of peeling paint. A couple of gator skins had been tacked over the worst spots.

The roof was a rusted patchwork of mismatched tin sheets. In one section, a metal garbage can had been battered flat and hammered down.

This place was as far from proud Haven as possible. I thought I'd seen poor. I was mistaken.

"That's where he lives?" Mel shuddered. "It's horrid."

Suddenly I regretted her seeing this, as if I'd betrayed a secret of Jackson's, which didn't make any sense.

"Evie, my car'll get stuck if I drive any farther. And it's not like we have our phones on us."

"Not *yet*. Just stay here, and I'll walk it. Be back with our stuff."

"What if he's not even here?"

I pointed out his motorcycle, parked under an overhang beside the rickety front porch. "That's his."

When I opened the car door, she said, "*Think* about this."

I had. The entire situation was so *unnecessary*. None of this had needed to happen. All because Jackson had stolen from me! He'd violated my privacy, had possibly read and heard my intimate exchanges with Brandon.

And he'd seen my drawings.

That freedom I'd vowed I would never take for granted? His actions were threatening it!

Remembering what was at stake made me slam the car door and venture forth. Yellow flies swarmed me, but I kept going, wending around tires, busted crab traps, cypress knees.

Closer to his house, there was no cut lawn, there wasn't even grass. In these parts, some folks who couldn't afford a lawnmower "swept" their yards, keeping them free of vegetation—and of snakes. His yard was a giant patch of hard-packed earth.

As I neared, I saw tools hanging from the porch roof. A machete and a saw clanked together in the growing breeze.

I crossed a dried-out depression in front of four wobbly-looking steps. The first stair bowed even under my weight. How did a boy as big as Jackson climb them?

There was no knocker on the unpainted plywood door, just a rusted lever to open it. The bottom was shredded in strips.

From when animals had scratched to get in?

With a shiver, I glanced back at the sky, saw the clouds were getting worse. I gazed at Mel in the distance, pensive in her car. *Maybe this is . . . stupid.*

No. I had to get that journal back. I found my knuckles rapping the wood. "Hello?" The door groaned open. "Mr. or Ms. Deveaux?" No answer. "I need to talk to Jackson," I called as I stepped into the house.

I saw no one inside but still got an eyeful. Just as bad as the outside.

The main living area was cramped, the ceiling hanging so low I wondered if Jackson had to duck to walk around. Dangling from it was a single lightbulb, buzzing like a bee.

The one window had been boarded up. The door to a room in the back was closed, but I heard a TV blaring from inside.

On the left wall was a small kitchen. Six fish lay cleaned beside a sizzling pan. Some kind of game was chopped in chunks, already breaded in cornmeal. Had Jack angled, trapped, or shot everything on that counter?

Why leave the stove on? "Jackson, where are you?" With a despairing eye, I took a closer look around the room.

Lining the wall to the right was a plaid couch, with cigarette burn holes pocking the arms. Frayed sheets had been spread over the sunken cushions.

His boots sat on the floor at the foot of the couch. *This is where he sleeps?*

My lips parted. He didn't even have his own room.

A *Spanish for Beginners* book lay on the floor, spine cracked and opened in the middle, with a worn copy of *Robinson Crusoe* beside it. That novel wasn't on our reading list. So he read for enjoyment? And wanted to speak another language?

I felt something tugging inside of me. As much as I thought of him as grown, he was just an eighteen-year-old boy who would have a boy's plans and dreams.

Maybe he imagined running away to Mexico or sailing away from this hellhole.

It struck me how little I really knew about him.

As my anger faded, I reminded myself that what little I knew, I *hated*. Still, I found myself trudging forward to turn off the stove before the place caught fire.

I nibbled my lip. *Where is he?* What if my sketchbook was at Lionel's? I didn't see any of the phones here either.

After I turned off the burner, I heard yelling from the back. Not the TV?

Suddenly a harsh drumming pelted the tin roof. I gave a cry of surprise, but that noise drowned it out. "Just the rain," I murmured to myself. "Drops on tin."

Finally!

Water started beading along bulging seams in the ceiling, dripping down to the floor, over the couch. Jackson would have nowhere dry to sleep tonight.

I jumped when stomping sounds shook the house, as if someone was bounding up a back set of stairs. When a door slammed in the back, the connecting door creaked open.

Morbid curiosity drew me closer. *One peek and I'll slip out....*

On a stained mattress, a middle-aged woman lay sprawled unconscious, her long jet-black hair a tangled halo around her head. She was nearly indecent, her robe hiked high up her legs. A rosary with glinting onyx beads and a small gothic cross circled her neck.

Her arm hung over the side, an empty bottle of bourbon on the floor just beneath her fingertips. A plate of untouched scrambled eggs and toast sat atop a box crate by the bed.

Was that Ms. Deveaux?

A tall, sunburned man in wet overalls came into view. He started pacing alongside the bed, yelling at her unconscious form, gesturing with one fist and his own liquor bottle.

Was the man her husband? Her boyfriend?

I knew I needed to leave, but I was riveted to the spot, could no more look away than I could quit breathing.

Then I saw Jackson on the other side of the bed, pulling her robe closed. Shaking her shoulder, he urgently muttered, *"Maman, reveille!"*

She slurred something but didn't move. The way Jackson gazed at her face, so protectively . . . I knew he'd cooked her that breakfast this morning.

When the drunk lumbered toward her, Jackson smacked the man's arm away.

Both began yelling in Cajun French. Even with what I understood, I could barely follow. Jackson was trying to kick him out, telling him never to return?

The man reached for Ms. Deveaux again. Jackson blocked him once more. Then the two squared off at the foot of the bed. Their voices got louder and louder, bellows of rage as they circled each other.

Did the idiot not see that glint in Jackson's eyes? The one promising pain?

Instead of heeding that warning, the man clutched the neck of his bottle, busting the bottom of it on the windowsill. Surprisingly fast, he attacked with the jagged end. Jackson warded off the blow with his forearm.

I saw bone before blood welled. I thrust the back of my hand against my mouth. *Can't imagine that pain!*

But Jackson? He merely smiled. *An animal baring its teeth.*

At last, the drunk clambered back in fear. Too late. Jackson launched his big body forward, his fists flying.

A stream of blood spurted from the man's mouth, then another, and still Jackson ruthlessly beat him. The strength in his towering frame was brutal, the wildness in his eyes . . .

Why couldn't I run? Leave this sordid place behind?

Leave these horrific *sounds* behind—the angry rain on tin, the woman's slurring, the drunk's grunts as Jackson landed blow after blow.

Then . . . one last punch across the man's jaw. I thought I heard bone crack.

The force of the blow sent the man twirling on one foot, drooling blood and teeth as he went down.

With a heartless laugh, Jackson sneered, *"Bagasse."*

Cane pulp. Beaten to a literal pulp. I covered my ears with my forearms, fighting dizziness.

Now that the man had been defeated, Jackson's wrath seemed to ebb. Until he slowly turned his head in my direction. His brows drew together in confusion. "Evangeline, what are you . . . ?"

He swept a glance around his home, as if seeing it through my eyes. As if seeing this hellhole for the first time.

Even after Jackson's display of raw violence, I couldn't stop myself from pitying him.

He must have seen it in my expression, because his face reddened with embarrassment. His confusion evaporated, that rage returning. His gaze was almost *blank* with it. *"Why in the hell did you come here?"* The tendons in his neck strained as he stalked toward me. *"You tell me why you're in my goddamned house!"*

I could only gape as I retreated. *Don't turn your back on him, don't look away. . . .*

"A girl like you in the Basin? *C'est ça coo-yôn! Bonne à rien!* Good for nothing but getting yourself in trouble!" I'd never heard his accent so thick.

"I—I—"

"Wanted a look at how the other half lives? That it?"

I backed across the front threshold, almost to the porch steps. "I wanted the journal you stole!"

Lightning flashed, highlighting the lines of fury on his face. Thunder boomed instantly, shaking the house so hard the porch rattled. I cried out and swayed for balance.

"The journal with all your crazy drawings? You come to take me to task!" When Jackson reached for me with that injured arm, I recoiled, scrambling backward into the pounding rain.

That loose step seemed to buckle beneath my foot; pain flared in my ankle.

I felt myself falling . . . falling . . . landing on my ass in a puddle. I gasped, spitting mud and rain, too shocked to cry.

Strands of wet hair plastered my face, my shoulders. I tried to rise, but the mud sucked me down. I swiped hair out of my eyes, coating my face with filth.

Blinking against the rain, I shrieked, "You!" I wanted to rail at him, to blame him for my pain, my humiliation. And all I could say over and over was *"You!"* Finally I managed to yell, "You disgust me!"

He gave a bitter laugh. "Do I? I didn't last night when you were wettin' your lips, hoping I'd kiss them, no. You wanted more of me then!"

My face flushed with shame. Then I remembered. "You tricked me so your loser friend could steal our stuff. You acted as if you liked me."

"You didn't seem to mind!" He raised his uninjured arm, shoving his fingers through his hair. "I heard your message to Radcliffe. You goan to kiss me? Then let that boy have you just days later?"

"Give me my journal!"

"Or what? What you goan do about it? The little doll got no teeth."

Frustration surged, because he was right. The Cajun had all the power; I had none.

Unless *I* could choke someone in vine or slice them to ribbons, like the red witch in my dreams?

As my nails began to transform, I felt something akin to the blissful unity that I'd shared with the cane. I was awash in an awareness of all the plants around me—their locations, their strengths and weaknesses.

Above Jackson's house, a cypress tree shifted its branches over me. In the distance, I sensed kudzu vines hissing in response, slithering closer to defend me.

And for a brief moment, I experienced an urge to show him who really had the power, to punish him for causing me pain.

Punish him? No, no! At once, I struggled to rein back the fury I'd unleashed.

"You want your drawings?" Jackson stormed inside, returning with my journal. "Have them!" He flung the notebook like a Frisbee. Pages went sailing out, all over the muddy yard.

"Nooo!" I cried out, watching them scatter, about to hyperventilate.

By the time I'd managed to crawl to my hands and knees, I was breathing so hard I choked and coughed on raindrops. I reached for the pages nearest me, but every handful of paper made a vision sear my mind.

Death. The bogeymen. The sun shining at night.

With each page, I jerked again and again, yelling up at him, "*I hate you!* You disgusting brute!" His handsome face hid seething violence.

Even though he'd been protecting his mother, he'd *liked* beating that man unconscious. Jackson had just proved how heartless a boy he truly was. *Bagasse . . .*

"HATE you! Never come near me again!"

He blinked at my face, his expression turning from murderous to disbelieving. He shook his head hard.

What was he seeing?

"Evie!" Mel cried. She'd come for me!

As she looped an arm around my shoulders to help me stand, she yelled at Jackson, "Stay away from her, you lowlife trash!"

With a last dumbstruck look at my face, he turned to stride away.

Just as he slammed inside that shack, my vines reached his porch. Mel was too busy checking me for injuries to see, but I watched them sway upright like cobras, waiting for me to command them.

I whispered, *"No."* They raced back into the brush as fast as plucked rubber bands. Then I told Mel, "I-I need these drawings. All of them."

Without a word, she dropped to her knees beside me.

Both of us in the mud, collecting my crazy.

"You're being so quiet," I said to Mel as she helped me up to my front porch. The rain was receding, the screen door open to the night breeze. We were both still coated with mud. "I hate when you go quiet."

On the way here, I'd told her about CLC, my visions, my mom, my gran—though not about the plants—finishing just as we'd pulled up.

Now, after my confession, I felt battered, like one of those dolls that always bounces back up when hit. But here was the thing—those silly dolls got hit all the more for it.

When will this day end? My bottom lip trembled as I fought off tears.

"I'm waiting for you to tell me what happened in the Cajun's shack," Mel said. "I mean, your expression was unforgettable—you were all like, *'Pa, I seen something behind the woodshed.'"*

"Maybe one day I'll tell you." Right now the memory was too raw.

"How come I'm the last to know you have visions? The woman who spawned you knew before me. And that hurts."

"I didn't want you to look at me differently." When we reached the door, I said, "I understand if you don't want to be friends anymore." I motioned for my backpack, stuffed full of sodden pages.

With a roll of her eyes, Mel handed over my bag. "And miss my opportunity to sell your disturbed little drawings online? No way, my freaky minx." She curled her arm around my neck, dragging me down so she could rub her knuckles in my muddy hair. "I'm going to be rich! So get me some more drawings that aren't soaking wet with Cajun funk all over them."

"Stop!" But amazingly, I was about to laugh.

"You sure you don't want me to come in?" Mel asked when she finally released me.

"I've got it," I told her. "I'm probably about to ugly-cry."

"Look, we'll figure out all of this tomorrow," Mel assured me. "But check this—you are not going back to that CLC place. Ever. If we have to, we'll run away together, get married in a civil union, and live off your art."

And there went my bottom lip again. "You've always been there for me, putting up with my crap."

Mel glared at me. "You're being *wank*, Greene. Cut out all this sentimental b.s. and ask yourself: What choice do I have? Hellooo. You're my *best* friend. Now, get inside before I take off the filter."

With a grave nod, I limped into the house, turning to wave as Mel drove off with her stereo blaring and her signature three-honk salute.

When I hobbled into the kitchen, Mom was making popcorn. "Hi, hon," she called over one shoulder, her tone cheerful. "Can you believe it rained—" Her eyes went wide at my appearance. "Evie! What happened to you?"

"I tripped in the mud. It's a long story."

"Are you hurt?"

I shrugged, gripping the strap of my backpack. Define *hurt*. "My ankle's a little sprained."

"I'll get some ice and Advil." Had Mom's attention darted past me to the door? "And then you can tell me what happened."

While she wrapped ice in a dishrag, I plunked myself down in a chair, keeping my bag of drawings close. "It's not a big deal, Mom."

As I debated how to explain away this mishap, the winds picked up, blowing through the screened door.

Though we'd gotten rain, the breeze felt hot and dry. Like a scarf out of the dryer rubbed against my cheek.

When it blew again and harder, Mom frowned. "Um, just let me check out the Weather Channel really quick." She grabbed the remote for our kitchen TV and turned it on.

The screen was divided between three harried-looking field reporters, the trio talking over each other. One of them was the guy who'd been all blasé while at ground zero for the last major hurricane.

So why was he sweating profusely now? "Sightings of bizarre weather phenomena in the eastern states . . . get a shot over my left shoulder . . . just look at those lights, folks . . . is that the *sun* rising?"

The second reporter looked like he hadn't blinked in a week. "Temperatures spiking . . . fires in the Northeast . . . there's no cause for panic," he said in a panicked voice. "Radiation spikes . . . reports of aurora borealis as far south as Brazil . . ."

The third guy's microphone shook in his trembling hand. "We've lost contact with our London, Moscow, and Hong Kong bureaus . . . all reported similar events"—he pressed his ear com—"what's that . . . New York? *DC?*" he said, his voice scaling an octave higher. "M-my family's in Wash—"

One by one, the feeds cut out. *Blip. Blip. Blip.*

"Mom?" I whispered. "What's going on?" *Why is your face paler than I've ever seen it?*

She glanced past me; her fingers went limp. The ice cubes clattered to the floor.

I lurched to my feet, my ankle screaming in protest. I was too scared to look behind me, too scared not to. Finally I followed Mom's gaze. Across the now-clear night sky, lights flickered.

Crimson and violet like Mardi Gras streamers.

I'd seen this very thing during the Fool Card's first appearance to me. It was the aurora borealis. The northern lights in Louisiana.

They were utterly mesmerizing.

As Mom and I both crept toward the front door, that hot wind intensified, beginning to howl, rattling the chimes around the farm. The horses shrieked in the barn. I could hear their hooves battering their stalls, wood splintering.

They sounded terrified—

But just look at those dazzling lights! I could stare forever.

From the east, the cane rustled. A mass of fleeing animals burst from the fields. Raccoons, possums, nutria, even deer. So many snakes erupted from the ditches that the front lawn shone and rippled.

A wave of rats surged. Birds choked the sky, tearing at each other or dive-bombing the ground. Feathers drifted in the winds.

But the lights! So magnificent they made me feel like weeping with joy.

And yet, I didn't think I should be looking at them. Had Matthew said something, warned me? I couldn't think, could only stare.

The massive Haven oaks groaned then, distracting my attention. Mom didn't seem to notice, but they were *moving*, tightening their rain-soaked limbs around us. They spread a shield of green leaves over our home, as if readying to defend it.

My cane seemed stunned, standing rigid, even in that wind. As if shell-shocked.

They know what's coming. They know why I should . . .

Turn away from the lights! "Mom, don't look at the sky!" I shoved her back from the door.

She blinked, rubbing her eyes, as though coming out of a trance. "Evie, what is that noise?"

A roar was building in the night, the loudest, most harrowing sound I'd ever imagined.

Yet Mom's demeanor grew icy cold. "We are not going to panic. But we will be locked inside the cellar within thirty seconds. Understood?"

The apocalypse . . . it was now. And Mel was out there alone.

"I have to call Mel!" Then I remembered she didn't have a phone. "If I drive across the property, I can catch her!"

Mom clenched my arm and swung me around toward the cellar.

"I'm not going down there without Mel! I have to get to her!"

I lunged for the front door, but Mom hauled me back, her strength unreal. "Get in the cellar NOW!" she yelled over the roar. "We can't risk it!"

The sky grew lighter—*hotter.* "No, no!" I shrieked, fighting her. "She'll die, she'll die, you know she will! I've seen this!"

"You both will if you go after her!"

I flailed against Mom, but couldn't break her hold. Arms stretched toward the front door, I sobbed, thrashing in a frenzy as she dragged me back to the cellar stairs.

When I clung to the doorway, she yanked on me, peeling my fingers from the doorjamb. "No, Mom! *P-please* let me go after Mel!"

Then came a shock of light. A blast of fire shook the ground. My eardrums ruptured—

A split second later, the force of the explosion hurled us down the stairs, the door slamming behind us.

THE HUNTER

Jackson Daniel Deveaux

A.k.a.: Jack Daniels, the Cajun, J.D., the general

Special Skills: Expert fighter with keen survival instincts and weapons knowledge. Self-defense, marksmanship, bowmanship.

Weapons: Crossbow, fists.

Before Flash: A transfer student at Sterling High in Louisiana, fresh from a cage-the-rage prison diversion program.

BASIN TOWN, LOUISIANA
(CAJUN COUNTRY)
DAY 0

"My decision is . . . yes. I'll spend the night with you."
Rewind.
"My decision is . . . yes. I'll spend the night with you."
Rewind.
"My decision is . . . yes. I'll spend the night with you."
Rewind.

EARLIER THAT DAY

When had Evangeline Greene gone from being Brandon's girlfriend to Evie, the girl who was going to drive me crazy?

I sat at the table with her drawing journal open, scrolling through Brandon's cell phone.

This morning she'd been calling it from her house phone. How could she not know her boyfriend's cell had been stolen? We'd pinched more than a dozen of them. I had Evie's as well, but hers was locked; Brandon's was wide open and chock-full of pictures and videos of her.

Ever since I'd gotten home from Haven last night, I'd looked through album after album.

The phone also had texts. I'd read them all now. With Brandon, she was flirty; she made fun of herself and could take a joke. The two of them had texted back and forth with so much ease—almost like their conversation had been planned.

Then nothing. As if she'd dropped off the face of the earth.

Over the summer, only a couple of texts had come—on the exact same day of the month, at the same time.

I scrolled to one picture from a year ago. She was on *my* father's yacht with Brandon. And no one had any idea I was the oldest son, the should-be heir.

She was sunbathing in a red bikini that heated my blood. I scrubbed my hand over my mouth. "Mercy me." I'd never looked at anything so pretty in my life.

The videos of her telling jokes and playing with a dog on a beach drew my attention too. She was so relaxed, so at home with herself.

Now she was . . . different.

I turned to her journal, full of grisly sketches. I didn't understand why she was drawing this eerie Goth shit now, but somehow I knew she hadn't been when those relaxed videos were taken.

In one of her drawings, the night sky was filled with fire. Fleeing rats and snakes made the ground look like it rolled. In another drawing, a thick vine squeezed a man to death, so hard his eyes popped from his skull.

The worst sketch was of a zombielike monster with filmy white eyes and leathery skin drinking blood from a victim's neck.

Why had Evie drawn these things? *I got to know, me.*

I didn't like puzzles. But deep down, I didn't think that was why she held my interest so strongly.

I ran the pad of my forefinger over the red ribbon I'd taken from her last night. Raising it to my face, I inhaled her scent, my lids growing heavy.

I stuffed the ribbon into my pocket right before Maman shuffled out from her room. She looked exhausted, and she'd lost more weight. Her threadbare robe swallowed her. *Goan to get her to eat more.*

She took one look at my face and said, "You met a *fille* you like." Her gray eyes livened up, until she reminded me of the Hélène Deveaux of old. When Maman was like this, I could more clearly remember the woman who'd read me *Robinson Crusoe* every night until I'd memorized the lines and would say them with her.

When I'd gotten older, she'd taught me to read on my own, telling me, "If you ever doan like where you are, open a book, and it'll take you somewhere else. It's a kind of magic, *cher*."

I smoothly closed Evie's drawing journal and stowed it in my backpack. "Maybe I have."

Maman's lips curled. Of course, my meeting a *fille* I liked was big news. Girls had always been interchangeable before. I'd never found one I'd even seen twice. I sure as shit had never obsessed over a girl like this.

Maman grabbed a mug, mixing bourbon with a splash of coffee. I didn't bother asking her to hold off. Was a time when I'd hidden bottles and money, but she'd always found a way to drink.

"Tell me about her." Maman settled into a chair at the table. "What's she look like?"

I hesitated, then admitted, "Pretty as the day is long. Blond hair and blue eyes." Short, curvy, smelled like a blossom.

Over the last week at school, I'd gotten close to her at every chance, going to my locker near hers after each class and watching her at lunch.

For the hour she'd slept in English one day, I hadn't taken my eyes off her. She'd drawn her brows and made a gasping sound, her pink lips parted and fingers clutching the desk.

Seeing her in the grip of a nightmare had affected me in strange ways. All of a sudden, I'd had a blistering need to kill whatever was scaring her. To punish whatever it was—just for *trying* to scare her.

A girl like that ought to have no fears.

Friday night I'd headed to the Sterling High football game with my crew. All that adoration for my dim-witted half brother had made me sick, but I'd choked back bile just to see her. She'd been in that cheer skirt. *Mere de Dieu*, I'd thought, *I could watch this all night.*

"What's her name?" Maman asked.

"Evangeline."

Maman smiled. "A good Cajun name. I'd ask if she's already head over heels for you, but I know the answer to that. All the *filles* in the Basin love my boy."

This one definitely didn't. "Evangeline *Greene*. From Sterling."

"Greene?" Maman's smile faded. "You're not talking about them Haven folks? Bad energy swirls around that place."

You got no idea. Last night, as I'd walked with Evie through the cane field, I could've sworn I'd heard . . . whispers. And those giant oak trees around the mansion had seemed to move in the flickering gaslight. Chills had skittered up my back. "That's her home."

"*Mais non*, you can't be with her."

"I ain't exactly *with* her." That girl did nothing but make *le misère* for me.

"But you want to be."

God, did I want to be.

"She haunting you?"

I exhaled. *"Ouais, elle me hante."* Yeah, she haunts me.

Maybe because she kept laughing at me. Maybe because she didn't *want* me to pursue her—a first for me.

More likely, it was because when I looked at her, everything in me lit up like never before. Whenever I was around her, for the first time in my life, I felt like I was right where I was supposed to be.

Maman's expression grew panicked. "*Non, non*, Jackson! You can't fall for that one. *Le cheval reste dans l'écurie, le mulet dans la savane.*" The horse lives in the stable, the mule in the pasture.

In other words, I should know my place.

"Doan do like I did with your father!" Jonathan Radcliffe.

The man had made her all kinds of promises—only to marry another woman, Brandon's mother. It should have been Maman living in that mansion, should have been her driving the Mercedes and having teas. It should have been her son playing quarterback as a crowd cheered.

I'd planned to hurt my brother. I would never have his fancy car, or his rich father, or his mansion. But when I'd seen a beautiful blonde leaning over to kiss him, I'd decided to steal his girl from him.

The best-laid plans and all that. Evie liked the rich ones. She must. That was the only thing Brandon had going over me.

Last night, she'd actually shown some curiosity about me, asking me a few questions. But at the end, we'd fought, my *jalousie* pushing me to hurt her. I'd succeeded, but she'd landed the parting shot: "You're a cruel, classless boy who gets off on other people's unhappiness. Brandon is twice the man you are. He always will be."

Twice the man. Even now my gut clenched.

I'd hated my brother before. Bitterly. But now it was even worse. 'Cause he had *her*.

I'd trade all the things Brandon took for granted, all that I'd coveted, for Evie.

Maman rose to top off her mug again. I was so uneasy, I nearly asked her to pour me one.

"You think you're goan to rub elbows up in that grand house with those fancy people?"

I *didn't* think that. I looked around at this shack, and I knew it was never going to be.

She returned to the table with her eyes watering. "I used to believe that. And look where I am now." Her tears spilled over.

I hated crying! Her tears usually wrecked me, but I was so pissed. "You're here 'cause you woan stop drinking, woan try!"

"Je fais de mon mieux." I'm doing the best I can. "I had my heart broken. The people in my family love once. You doan know what it's like to feel as if something's missing from your chest every second of every day. You mark my words, boy. You doan belong with a *fille* like that. Worst thing you can do is dream."

"Who *do* I belong with, then? Maybe I should find me the female equivalent of Vigneau?" That was Maman's current beau, an asshole who could outdrink us all and liked to take his anger out on her.

A couple of weeks ago, he'd sent her home from the *bourré* hall with a black eye. I burned to make him pay for that, but if I violated the terms of my parole, they'd ship me to Angola Prison. The money I made poaching would disappear. Maman would starve without me.

She swiped her sleeve over her face and finished her mug. "It's too late for you, *non*? This Evangeline has already set her claws. You better hope she wants you back."

Evie had craved my kiss last night before we'd been interrupted. When she'd wetted her lips and gazed up at me, I'd never wanted a kiss more.

Instead, she'd kissed my brother. *Brandon is twice the man you are. . . .*

Maman tilted her head at me, reading my expression. "Oh, Jack. *Mon pauvre fils.*" My poor son.

Even my mother pitied me.

I stuffed Brandon's phone in my pocket. "Goan to check my traps, me." I rose and headed outside without a look back.

Best I could do would be to leave this place. Sick of being pitied.

I'd just reached my makeshift pier when the cell phone rang. The caller ID read: *Greene.* I was tempted to answer it, but let it ring instead. This time she left a voice mail. I played it.

Evie's voice was shaky. "Hey, Brand, I hope everything's okay. Starting to worry." She didn't know we'd lifted the phones! "Last night, about our conversation . . . we got interrupted—when you went off to save the day for me. And I just wanted to tell you my decision." She paused.

Decision? I'd heard her and Brandon at her locker talking about this upcoming weekend. She was supposed to let him know if she would stay the night with him.

My eyes widened. If she would *sleep* with him! I didn't breathe as I waited for her to continue.

"My decision is . . . yes. I'll spend the night with you next weekend. I . . . I'm . . ." *She's what???* "Um, call me. At home."

My heart felt like it'd stop.

Then fury welled inside me. Goddamn it, Brandon had won again! I almost threw the phone in the bayou.

Clotile found me that night, nursing a bottle of Jack Daniels and pacing the shack, blood from my arm soaking through a towel.

She pulled the cloth aside and whistled in a breath. The slash had opened the flesh all the way down to the bone. "Eck! What the hell happened?"

"I had me a fucked-up day." Starting from this morning—my exchange with Maman, and Evie's message—all the way to the shit storm at sunset.

Vigneau had come to minutes ago, staggering away from the house, leaving a good many of his teeth behind. Evie had left not long before. . . .

Clotile raised her brows. "Looks it."

When Maman muttered drunkenly from the next room—"*Jonathan*"—I wondered if I'd lose my mind.

I gazed down at my sister. "I'm strangling here." Earlier I'd gotten on my bike to go somewhere—*anywhere* away from this shack—but I hadn't been able to throttle the motorcycle with my injured arm.

"You can tell me about it on the way," Clotile said. "I stole *ma mère*'s truck. Taking you to Doc's. Come on, you."

I'd been to Doc's enough, back when Maman's beaux had gotten rough with me and I hadn't been big enough to fight back. For years, the man had taken care of any injury I could see. For anything I *couldn't* see, I went to the parish emergency room. Head. Ribs. Kidney.

Driving to Doc's was a luxury. I used to have to walk an hour each way.

I wasn't relishing the stitches I'd need. But if I couldn't ride my motorcycle . . . "*Ouais.* Let's go." Bottle in hand, I followed Clotile out.

When I spied footprints in the mud, I winced. Why hadn't I helped Evie? I'd never treated a *fille* so bad.

Clotile and I climbed into the truck, and she didn't waste any time, skidding out, then flying down the highway. She didn't care for her good-for-nothing mother, and she damn sure didn't care about the woman's truck. "Who cut you?"

"Vigneau."

"I hope you did him one better."

I raised my bottle, took a slug. "*Mais yeah.* But if he goes to the cops, are they goan to believe I was defending Maman?" I hadn't just violated the terms of my parole; I'd committed the same offense. "I *tried* not to fight that *fils de putain*."

In the program I'd been forced to attend, they'd emphasized getting the hell away when a fight was brewing. I'd tried to wake up *ma mère* and get her out of the house, but she'd been blind drunk—'cause she was upset over me.

Over *me* becoming like *her*.

I adjusted the towel. Blood kept soaking through the material. "And then... Evangeline Greene showed up." Wearing the diamond necklace Brandon had given her.

No matter how many times I'd listened to her phone message over the day, her answer to Brandon always remained the same.

Yes.

All afternoon, I'd felt like a sickness had stolen over me. I'd walked around in a daze—mindlessly checking my traps, starting dinner, right up to my fight with Vigneau. And then she'd appeared, looking so damned beautiful.

Clotile cast me a shocked glance. "Showed up at your place?"

I nodded. "Inside. She saw the whole fight. Saw *ma mère*." Who'd been passed out in bed with an empty bottle nearby.

I'd gazed around my home, seeing it through Evie's eyes. Then I'd read her expression. She had ... pitied me.

My skin had *burned* from shame, like fire licking at me. I'd been choking on it.

I still was.

Clotile asked, "Why'd Evie come?"

"She wanted her things back." For some reason, I held off telling Clotile about Evie's drawings.

"Like those sketches? Lionel told us she drew crazy stuff."

Then her secret was out. I shrugged.

Clotile slid me a look. "And I'm sure you calmly escorted her out after returning her things."

"*Non.* I was yelling at her, and she was backing out onto the porch. She fell on the bad step and busted her ass in the mud." She'd screamed that I *disgusted* her. "I threw the pages of that journal out into the yard."

Clotile's lips parted. "And you thought *you* were having a fucked-up day?"

I sank back in the seat, drinking. "Not my finest moment." After that, I'd stomped back inside, finding a towel for my arm and a bottle of whiskey for my pride.

As Evie and her friend—who'd made sure to call me "lowlife trash"—had knelt in the mud to pick up every single page, I'd paced that tiny shack, hating it, hating my new school, hating my existence.

Most of all I hated Evie, all the more 'cause I wanted her so goddamned bad. I took another draw from my bottle to numb the pain—but not in my arm.

Just to make the night weirder, when Evie had been screaming at me, I'd seen things that couldn't be right. Like something had been . . . *glowing* on her face.

I shook away the thought, taking another slug.

"Why were you so mean to her, Jack? You've never been unkind to a *fille* a day in your life."

When I'd first seen Evie and looked into her eyes, for a split second everything in me had gone from full-on chaos to something like . . . peace. Christ, that feeling was addictive. So how was I going to live without it? "She's got me twisted up inside."

You doan belong with a fille like that. Maman was right. I was wanting something that would never be.

Damn it, my arm was still bleeding all over everything. I took another swig; Doc wasn't generous with painkillers.

After losing his medical license for drinking on the job or something, he'd set up a taxidermy outfit in his basement, but ended up splitting the area for an illegal patch-up shop.

He'd nailed plywood over the basement windows to keep the place cool and dark for tanning, which meant it wasn't exactly sterile down there. The air always smelled like paint, glue, and mothballs.

I pictured the good-natured old doctor, imagining his reaction to my arm. He would tsk over the slash, his ill-fitting dentures rattling around in his mouth, then say what he always did: "Coo-wee! Dat's a bad one. Boy, doan you know how to *run*?"

For payment, I brought him any extra gators I caught, dodging the wildlife officers so he didn't have to.

Clotile said, "Will you finally admit you want that girl for more than revenge?"

I hesitated, then nodded. "Doan matter now though, does it?" There was no way in hell I was ever going to be with her. No way.

I would never kiss her, never take her to bed. She'd never tell me silly jokes and laugh with me. I clenched the throat of my bottle.

Clotile sped up to make a yellow light, then said, "Brandon tried to kiss me last night."

"You're serious?" My half brother was used to getting everything he wanted. He had a girl like Evangeline Greene, his for the taking, and he wasn't true to her. I'd always known he was an idiot—this just confirmed it.

Yet she'd called him twice the man I was.

"I barely wriggled out of his grasp," Clotile said. "When do I get to tell him he might be my brother?" Maman wasn't the only Basin woman Jonathan Radcliffe had bedded. But Clotile's mother couldn't be a hundred percent certain Radcliff was the father, not like Maman.

Maybe I should've sued for paternity. If I had money like Brandon, would *I* be giving Evie diamonds and looking forward to sleeping with her in a week?

Christ, I'd be counting down the seconds. "Hold off for now," I told Clotile. "Lemme think on things tomorrow."

As we drove through the Basin, I gazed out the window. Poverty. Such a dirty word. Those Sterling kids didn't know what it was like to *want*. To have this deep strangling need inside so powerful it was like rage.

Mix rage with want. That was me.

"You doan need a *fille* anyway," Clotile pointed out. "You're goan to Mexico soon."

The second I was off parole. Once I quit school, I wouldn't likely cross paths with Evie ever again.

My usual restlessness seized me. I needed to get out of the Basin, or I would end up like Maman. "You sure you want to stay?"

Clotile gave me a firm nod. "We got a plan."

I would send money, and she'd look after *ma mère*. "I've been burning to leave this place, but that girl . . ." Something in me balked hard when I thought of never seeing Evie. She would be leaving for college in two years. Wasn't like we'd be going the distance.

She was done with me.

And I'd have to show up at school tomorrow or she would figure I'd stayed home with my tail between my legs. To hell with that. I'd go with my shoulders squared and hit on every girl but her.

As Clotile pulled up to Doc's place, she said, "For what it's worth, Jack, I liked her."

I scowled. "'Cause she waved and smiled at you once."

Clotile shrugged. "More than anyone else did."

***

Doc's basement lights went out mid-stitch.

Total dark, with a curved needle lodged in the lip of my wound. *Feel like a fish on a line, me.*

He cussed up a storm. "Damn that electric line. If a dog so much as pisses on the power pole, my lights go out."

Welcome to Cajun country.

He blindly dragged the needle through. "I got me a backup generator for my freezers. But I can't see nothing, no. Clotile, can you get to my workbench? There's a flashlight."

Something crashed in the dark. "Ow! *Non!*"

I remembered my new phone. "Here." I fired it up, giving off enough light for Doc to get to his bench and for Clotile to grab a seat near me.

"Stay put, son." Doc waved his flashlight. "I'll be right back to close dat arm up."

"Ain't goan nowhere." Once he'd made it to the stairs, I shone the light on my arm. He'd finished up one layer of sutures and was nearly done with the second.

Sure enough, he'd looked at my injury and said, "Coo-wee! Boy, you goan to learn how to run one of these days." He'd also checked out my taped fingers. Vigneau's teeth had sliced up my knuckles.

I'd just powered down the phone to save the battery when some rumble sounded from upstairs.

"Damn," Clotile said. "That generator could wake the dead, *non*?"

Minutes dragged by, and Doc still hadn't returned. Uneasy, I flicked the phone back on. "Something ain't right." My self-preservation instincts were honed razor sharp. I could usually tell when shit was about to hit the fan.

I hunted for scissors, then snipped the thread in my arm. When I rose, I lurched from the booze and blood loss. "Goan to check things out, me."

Clotile nodded. "I'm coming too."

I staggered up the stairs, with her right behind me. Opening the basement door, I yelled, "Doc? Where you at?" At the end of the long hallway, his front door was wide open. A hot, bone-dry wind rushed inside, hitting my face. He lived on the bayou front—where was the mugginess?

From here, I could see down his walkway. He stood motionless on the sidewalk, gazing up at something.

Other people along the shore stared skyward too.

When I strode down the hallway, Clotile followed, peeking past me. "What're they gawking at?"

Doc's pecan trees blocked my view of the sky. "Doan know." A light began to glow over the water.

"You think it's a *fifolet*?" A swamp light.

"Peut-être." Maybe. "If it is . . ." I trailed off when a doe bounded down the street right past Doc. He didn't react, just kept staring up.

Then came more animals, a parade of them fleeing from the east. Dogs, coyotes, rats, nutria.

I swallowed. One of Evie's sketches had been of fleeing animals.

In a hushed tone, Clotile said, "Something bad's coming."

That rumbling sound we'd been hearing got louder and louder until it was more like a roar. "A twister maybe? Christ, I left Maman passed out!"

"If a tornado's cropping up here, it probably woan reach your place."

For true. Still . . . "I gotta get to her. Give me your keys."

"*Jamais.*" Never. "We need to stay down in the basement." Clotile backed toward it, yanking on my good arm.

That mysterious light grew even more intense, like the bayou was trying to catch fire. And that roar . . .

I said, "Ain't a tornado, no." That roar *could* wake the dead. Seemed like it was ringing in the end of days.

The apocalypse.

I burned to get to Maman, but I got the sense I wouldn't make it to the truck.

"We got to hunker down, Jack!"

"Not without Doc." I pulled free of Clotile, then hurried toward the front door. "Get your ass inside, Doc!" From here I could see the sky. *My God.* Past him was the rising sun, like a ball of fire.

From the basement doorway, Clotile screamed, "Come back here! Please!"

I yelled, "*Allons-y*, Doc! Now—" A flash of light exploded like a bomb. Fingers of fire stretched over the bayou, about to reach us. *"DOC!"* I'd never get to him in time.

He finally shook himself and turned to me. Meeting my eyes, he mouthed: *Run, boy.*

For once, I did. I lunged for the basement door, yanking it closed behind me.

Clotile cried, "Down here!"

When the knob seared my hand, I leapt down the stairs. The building groaned, dust raining over us in the pitch dark.

Clotile blindly reached for me. "I-I'm scared."

So the hell was I. "We're goan to be okay." I took her hand.

"What happened to Doc?"

"I think . . ." How to explain what I'd just seen? "There was all this fire, and he told me to run. I doan see how he could've . . . lived through that."

"You think we got bombed? Or maybe it's the Rapture?"

"I doan know, me." All I knew was Maman was in her bed, defenseless as a baby.

"I'm done waiting," I told Clotile after pacing that dark basement for hours. Nothing else I could've done. We'd tried to call 911—and anyone else we knew—but couldn't get a connection.

I was gut-sick with worrying. And I hated myself 'cause I was also worrying about someone who should've meant *nothing* to me.

I'd thought of Evie more than I'd thought of my podnas Lionel, Gaston, and Tee-Bo. Once this was over and I'd gotten Maman safe somewhere, I'd ride to Haven.

"Just a little while longer." Clotile had insisted on bandaging up my arm, but I'd assured her that would be the least of our worries. "Please. It can't be safe out there."

We'd heard what sounded like an inferno outside, the entire Basin gone up in flames. There'd been more crashes and glass shattering. Doc's entire building had quaked.

And always, always there was the smell of smoke.

But the sounds were fading.

Clotile asked, "What if there's . . . radiation or something?"

"Ain't like I was goan to live a long life anyhow. You stay here. I'll go pick up Maman, check on some podnas, then I'll come back for you."

"You ain't leaving without me."

"Fine. Come on, you." By the light of that phone, we climbed the stairs again. I brushed the doorknob. Cool to the touch.

I opened up cautiously, easing the door back, and scented the air. To hell with it. I stepped out, glass cracking beneath my boots.

Every window had been shattered, the frames still smoking. We crept toward the front door.

Doc's pecan trees were charred stumps. His mulberry bushes had disappeared. Black streaks slashed over the bricks of his house. Other houses in the neighborhood were burning.

Next door, all that remained of a larger wooden home were cinders and a scorched Virgin Mary statuette; I crossed myself.

"Where are all the trees?" Clotile asked, sounding stunned as she surveyed the destruction.

I didn't see a single one. I swallowed. "Gone."

"You think there'd be some people around."

"Most everybody was outside when the fire hit." We reached the sidewalk, found a gray pile of ash. "Doc was standing right here." I toed the small mound, and my heart started to thunder.

Clotile wheezed in a breath. "A-are those what I think they are?"

Doc's dentures. *"Ouais."* I surveyed the street. More of those piles dotted the blistered pavement.

She whispered, "Those ... were people."

When I gazed out over the waterfront, my mind nearly turned over. "No water. It's all dried up." Only cracked mud remained. Blackened metal barges listed in the muck. The skeletons of shrimp boats still burned. "I can't be seeing right. Tell me ... tell me I'm on a bad bender, me. And I ain't seeing this."

Clotile shook her head, her face pale. "It's gotta be a nightmare."

"Need to get to Maman." We headed to the truck. The exterior was charred, but looked okay otherwise. Clotile tossed me the keys, and we climbed in the cab.

When the engine wouldn't turn over, I beat the steering wheel with frustration.

She put her hand on my shoulder. "Hey, we'll find us another one."

I eased off. I needed to keep my calm and focus. I nodded, and we got out to look. A lot of cars had been wrecked. Some were stalled out, right in the street. We tried a few of them, but none of them would crank.

I grated, "We're walking it." Wouldn't be the first time.

Along the road, we didn't meet another soul, but we passed more piles of ash.

Clotile stumbled. "Jack, we gone to hell?"

I helped her along. "Just . . . just keep walking, you." Could Maman have survived? The structures that had once had the most tree cover fared best; thick cypress boughs had stretched out over my shack. And it'd been soaked from the earlier downpour.

Maybe she'd lived.

My traitorous thoughts turned to Evie. Big oaks had surrounded Haven. Could she have made it from my place to hers before that flash of light? Before the fire? Had I gotten her killed . . . ? *Keep it together, Jack.*

For the last mile to my home, Clotile and I ran. I careened into my yard ahead of her, slowing in shock.

The cypress trees were stumps. The shack had collapsed, was just a mound of smoldering wood, covered with sheets of scorched tin. "Ah, God, Maman!" I sprinted to the pile, then yanked at the metal.

"Hélène!" Clotile called, hurrying over to help.

"Answer us, Maman!"

"Jack?" came a muffled reply from somewhere under the heap.

My eyes shot wide. "I'm here!" I tore at the boards like a madman, pitching them to the side. "Goan to get you free. Are you hurt? Anything broken?"

"Non." Her hand waved between boards.

I hauled debris away, enough to ease her out from under a heavy rafter, freeing her.

She threw her arms around me. "Jack! I knew you'd come for me."

"Thank God you're all right!" I drew back to brush mud off her face, frowning at the roughness of her cheek. Her skin felt leathery. And her cracked lips bled. "What's happened to you, Maman?" Her eyes were filmy, her gray pupils lighter, almost like chalk.

I fought a dawning recognition. She reminded me of . . . the creatures Evie had sketched.

I shared a glance with Clotile, who shook her head in confusion.

"I doan know." Maman's rosary was stark against her weathered neck. "I feel so strange, me." She tried to lick her battered lips.

"We're goan to get you to a doctor in the next parish over." The next state over, if we had to. Somebody would be able to help her.

She clutched my shoulders, her nails digging in. Her eyes seemed to be lightening even more, her skin getting worse by the second. "Oh, Jack, I never been so thirsty in all my days."

So why was her gaze locked . . . on my throat?

Find out what happens to Jack and many of these characters in the next pulse-pounding installment of the Arcana Chronicles: *Arcana Rising*, coming August 15, 2016.

Turn the page for a sneak peek!

ARCANA RISING

Losses mount and deadly new threats converge in the next action-packed tale of the Arcana Chronicles by #1 *New York Times* best-selling author Kresley Cole.

WHEN THE BATTLE IS DONE . . .

The Emperor unleashes hell and annihilates an army, jeopardizing the future of mankind—but Circe strikes back. The epic clash between them devastates the Arcana world and nearly kills Evie, separating her from her allies.

AND ALL HOPE IS LOST . . .

With Aric missing and no sign that Jack and Selena escaped Richter's reach, Evie turns more and more to the darkness lurking inside her. Two Arcana emerge as game changers: one who could be her salvation, the other her worst nightmare.

VENGEANCE BECOMES EVERYTHING.

To take on Richter, Evie must reunite with Death and mend their broken bond. But as she learns more about her role in the future—and her chilling past—will she become a monster like the Emperor? Or can Evie and her allies rise up from Richter's ashes, stronger than ever before?

1

Death kept taking me farther from Jack. I stretched my arms out, fingers splayed toward the heat. "He can't be dead." I sobbed. "Can't. NO, NO, NOOOO!"

"You want to follow the mortal? Get your revenge first. The Emperor mocks your pain."

I could hear that fiend in my head—laughing.

The red witch exploded inside me, a force that could never be contained. I shrieked, "You will PAY!"

As the Emperor laughed, Death murmured in my ear, "I have your grandmother, *Sievā*. That was the gift I spoke of. We'll teach you how to kill the Emperor. You'll avenge Deveaux."

"Don't you understand? Jack's not DEAD!" I screamed that over and over. "He's alive!"

With my mind teetering on the brink, I spied something in the skies above us. I gaped, disbelieving.

Real? Unreal? Just before oblivion took me down, a mountain of water curled over our heads, racing toward that hell of flames.

Circe's towering wave. Taller than a skyscraper.

—*Quake before me!*—

—*Terror from the abyss!*—

Richter and Circe's calls boomed in my mind, jolting me back from the blackness.

"Come!" Aric snatched me into his arms and sprinted from the clash. "When they meet, the blast and then the flood . . ."

I stopped fighting him; the need to turn Richter's laughter into screams clawed at me, which meant I had to survive.

Aric gave a sharp whistle, and a horse's nickering answered. Thanatos. With me secure in his arms, Aric leapt into the saddle, and spurred the warhorse into a frenzied gallop.

We all but dove down a slope, then charged up the next.

I gazed over Aric's shoulder as that tidal wave crested above Richter's lake of lava.

Heaving breaths, riding faster than humanly possible, Aric kept Thanatos at a breakneck pace. Up another mountain face. Down its slope—

Circe struck.

A hiss like a giant beast's. A detonation like a nuclear bomb.

The shock wave was so loud my ears bled. As loud as the roar preceding the Flash.

The air grew hotter and hotter. The ground rocked as a blast of scalding steam chased us.

BOOM! The force sheared the top off the mountain just behind us. Boulders crashed all around as we careened into yet another valley. Still we rode.

Aric grated, "Surge comes next."

The ground quaked from the weight of an ocean of water. I could hear the surge shooting toward us. *"Aric!"*

He got as far as he dared, as high as he could. "Hold on." Clutching me tight, he dropped from Thanatos who kept running.

Behind the cap of another mountain, Aric braced for impact. He wedged his metal gauntlet between boulders, wrapping his other arm around me.

Gaze locked on mine, he yelled, *"I'll never let you go!"* We each sucked in a breath.

The searing water hit. The explosive impact ripped me from his chest, but he caught my arm, clenching his fingers above my elbow.

172

Death's grip. The ungodly force of the flood. My watery scream . . .
Aric never did let me go—
My arm . . . gave way.
Separated.

CPSIA information can be obtained
at www.ICGtesting.com
Printed in the USA
LVHW041703170419
614532LV00001B/148